SEND FOR A SUPERHERO!

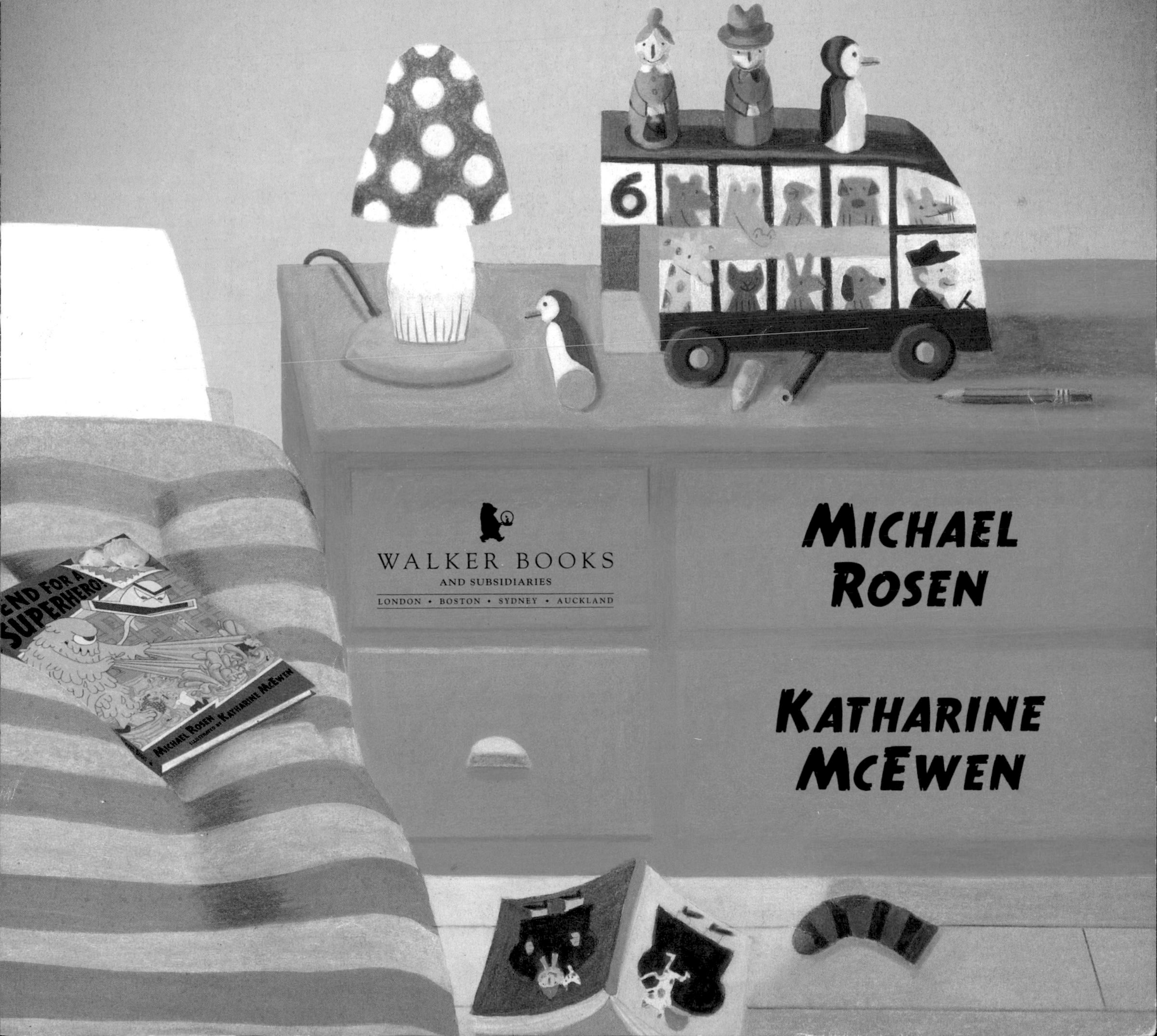

SEND FOR A SUPERHERO!
MICHAEL ROSEN
KATHARINE McEWEN
6

MICHAEL ROSEN

KATHARINE McEWEN

WALKER BOOKS
AND SUBSIDIARIES
LONDON • BOSTON • SYDNEY • AUCKLAND

It was bedtime and Dad was reading
Emily and little Elmer a story.

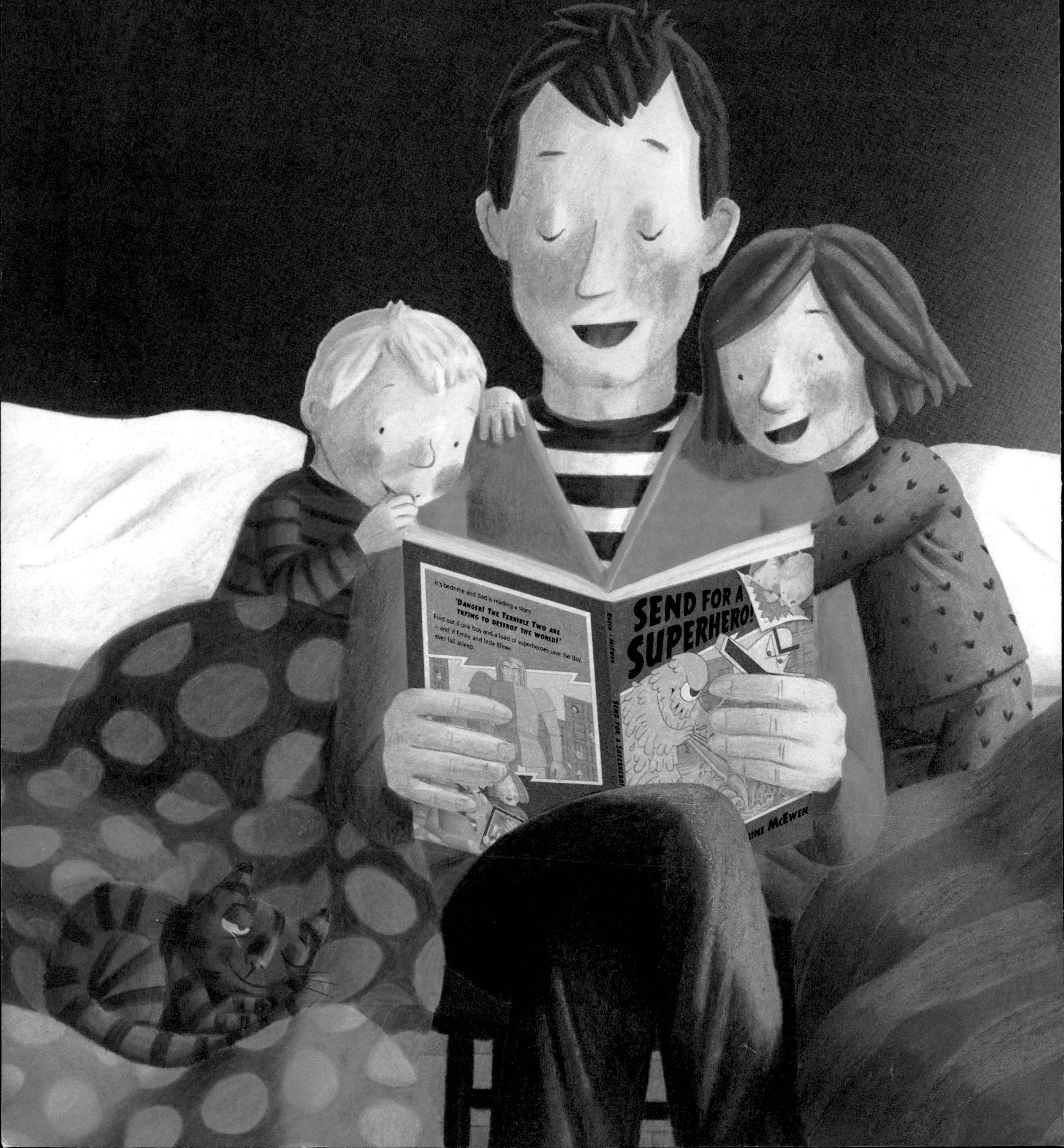

It's bedtime and dad is reading a story:
'DANGER! THE TERRIBLE TWO ARE TRYING TO DESTROY THE WORLD!'
Find out if one boy and a load of superheroes save the day, – and if Emily and little Elmer ever fall asleep.
ROSEN • MCEWEN
SEND FOR A SUPERHERO!
SEND FOR A SUPERHERO!
RINE MCEWEN

"Danger!" Dad began. "The Terrible Two are trying to destroy the world!"

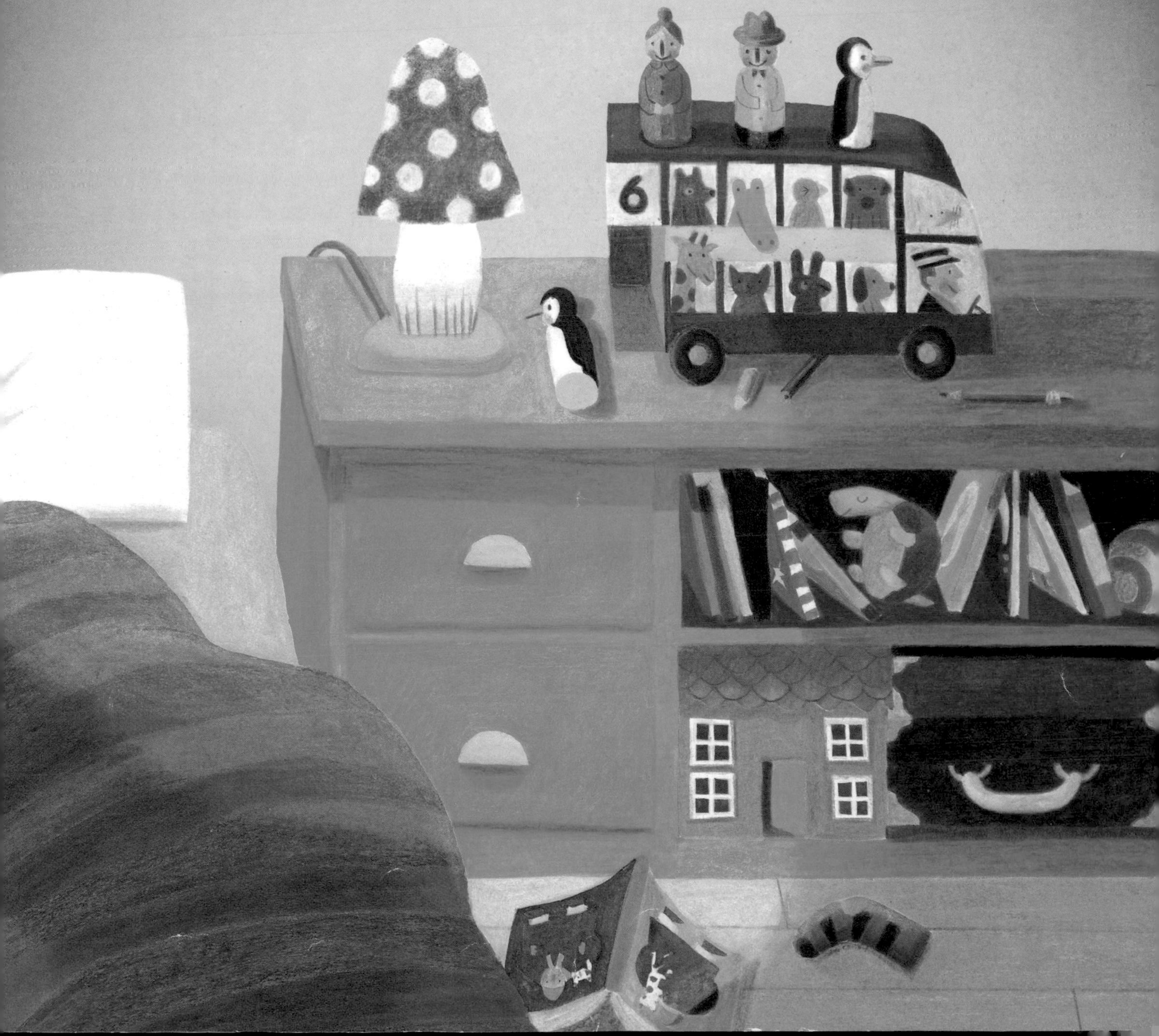
6

"Who are the Terrible Two?" said Elmer.

"Look," said Dad, "there's Filth... He pours muck and slime over everything."

"And there's Vacuum," said Emily.

"He can suck money and jewels and treasure out of people's pockets, out of drawers, even out of banks," said Dad.

"Wow!" said Elmer.

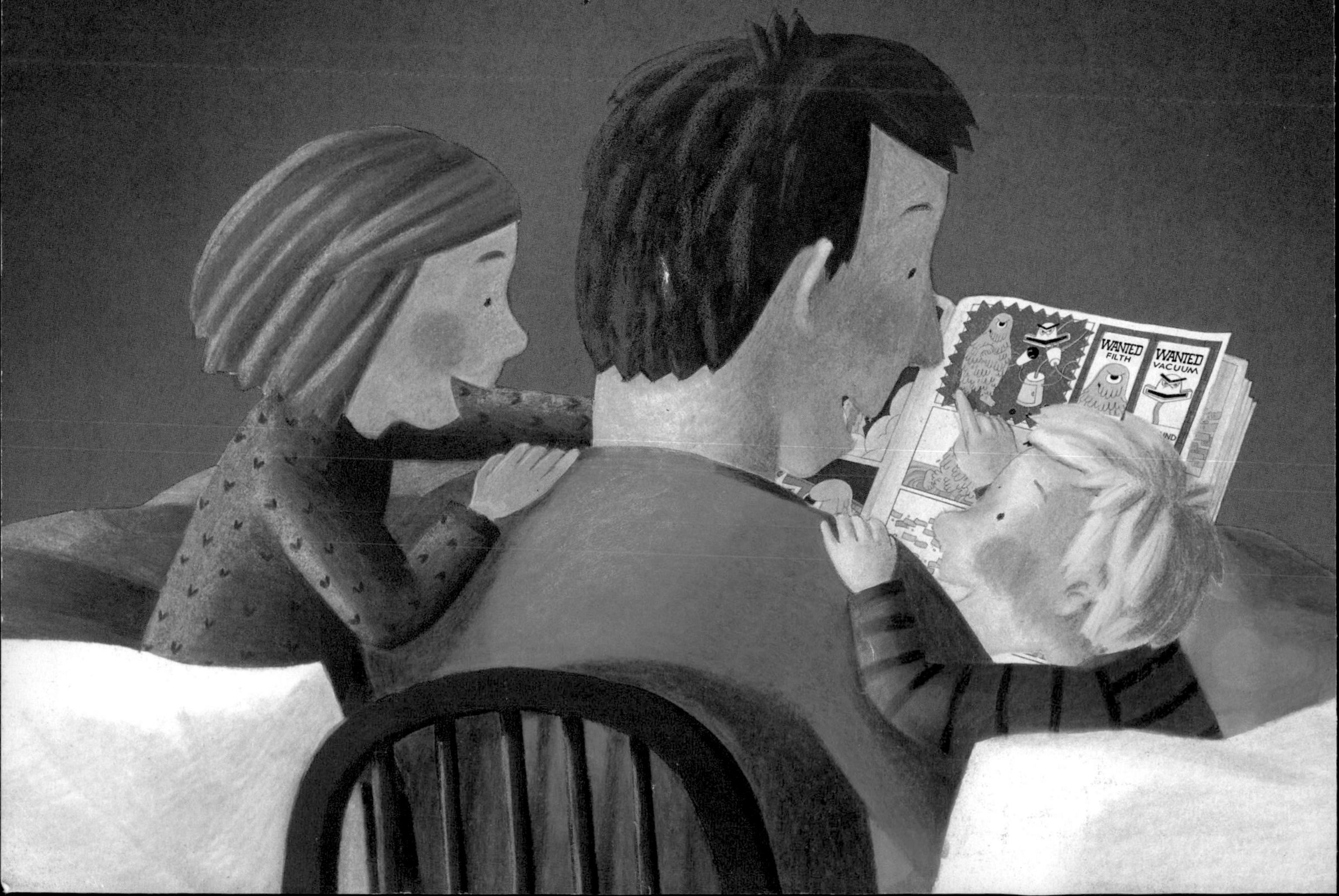
WANTED
FILTH
WANTED
VACUUM

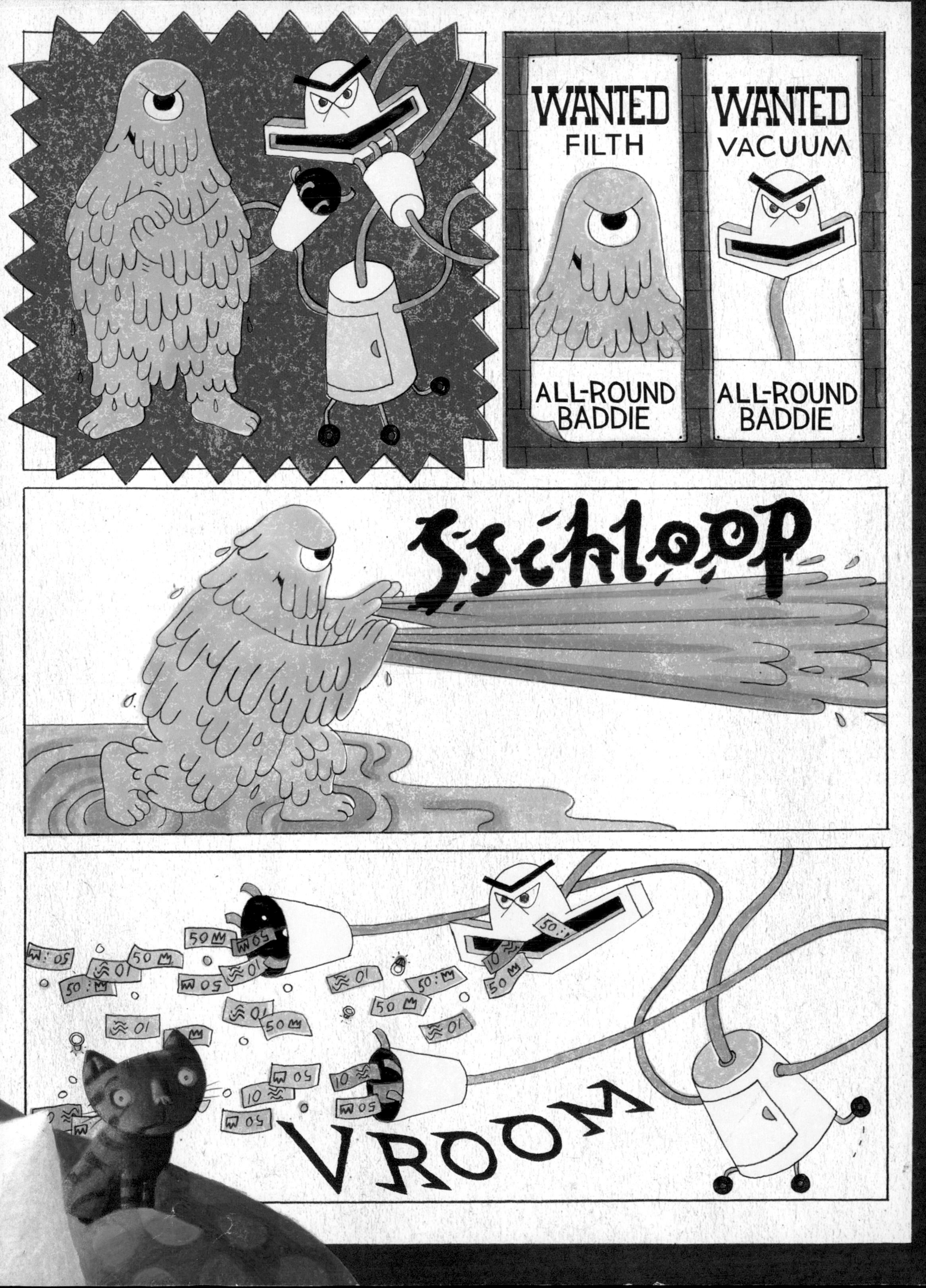
WANTED
FILTH
ALL-ROUND BADDIE
WANTED
VACUUM
ALL-ROUND BADDIE
Sschloop
VROOM

Dad went on...

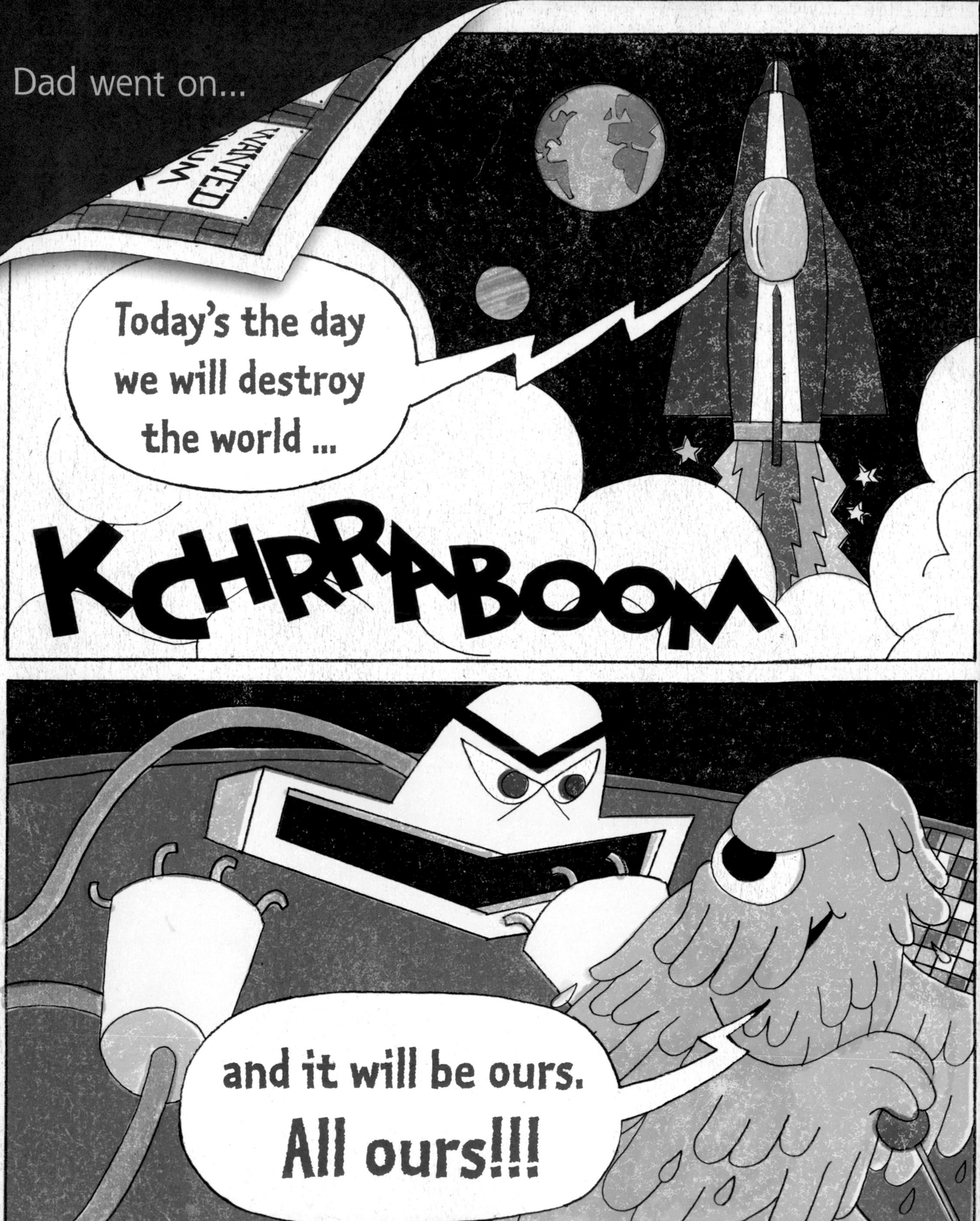
WANTED
Today's the day we will destroy the world ...
KCHRRABOOM
and it will be ours.
All ours!!!

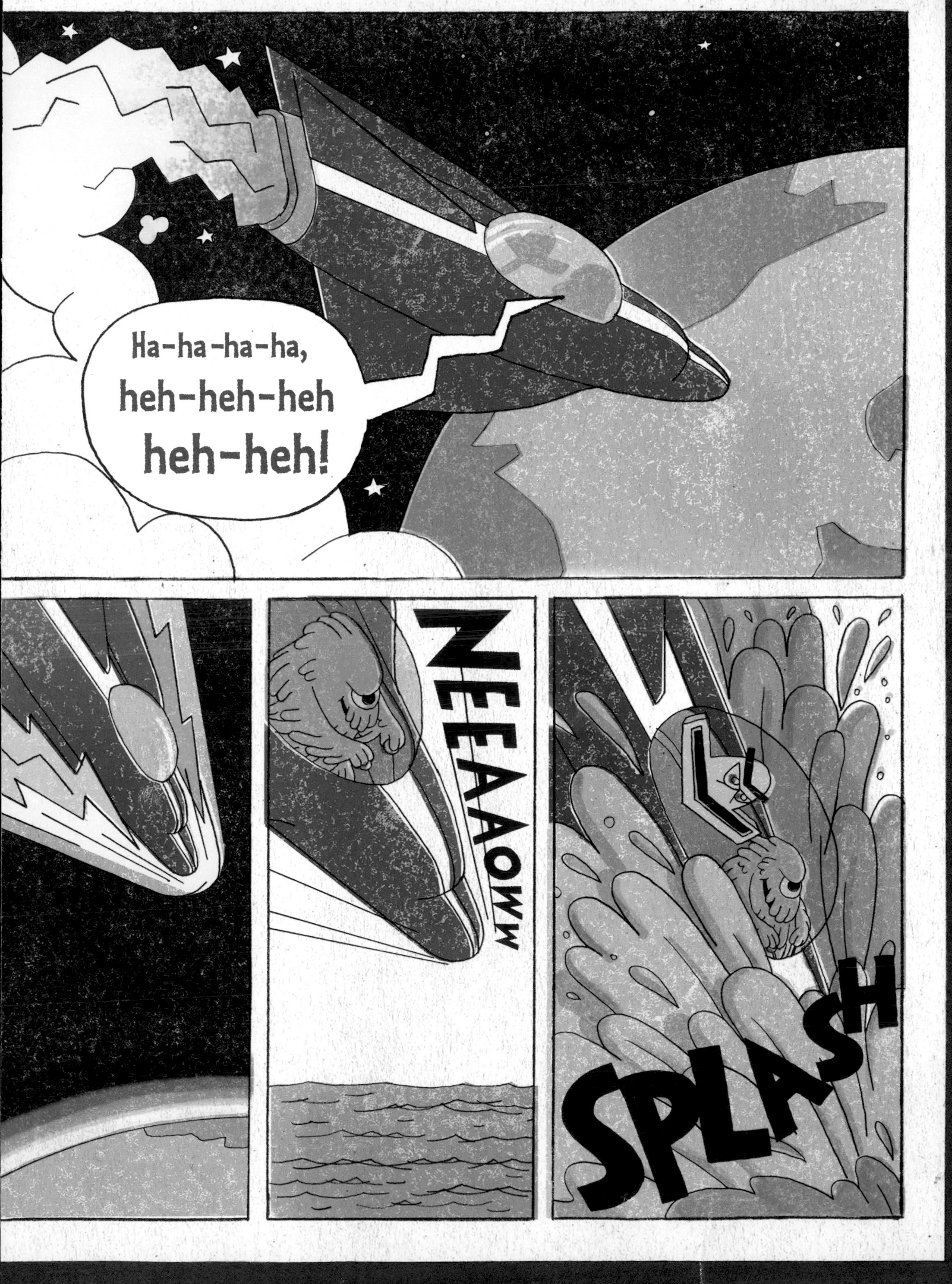

Ha-ha-ha-ha,
heh-heh-heh
heh-heh!
NEEAAAOWW
SPLASH

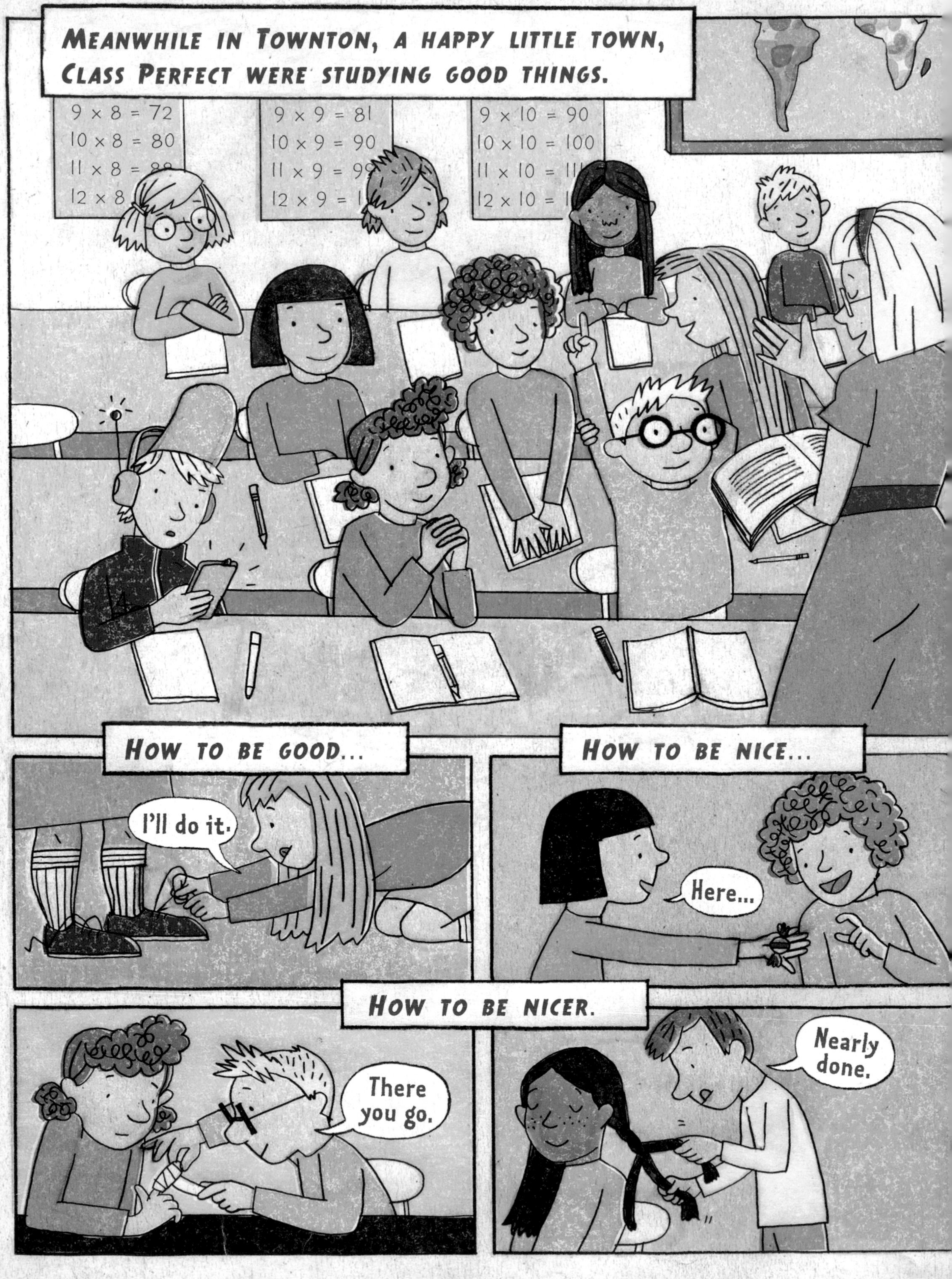
MEANWHILE IN TOWNTON, A HAPPY LITTLE TOWN, CLASS PERFECT WERE STUDYING GOOD THINGS.
9 × 8 = 72
10 × 8 = 80
9 × 9 = 81
10 × 9 = 90
9 × 10 = 90
10 × 10 = 100
HOW TO BE GOOD...
I'll do it.
HOW TO BE NICE...
Here...
HOW TO BE NICER.
There you go.
Nearly done.

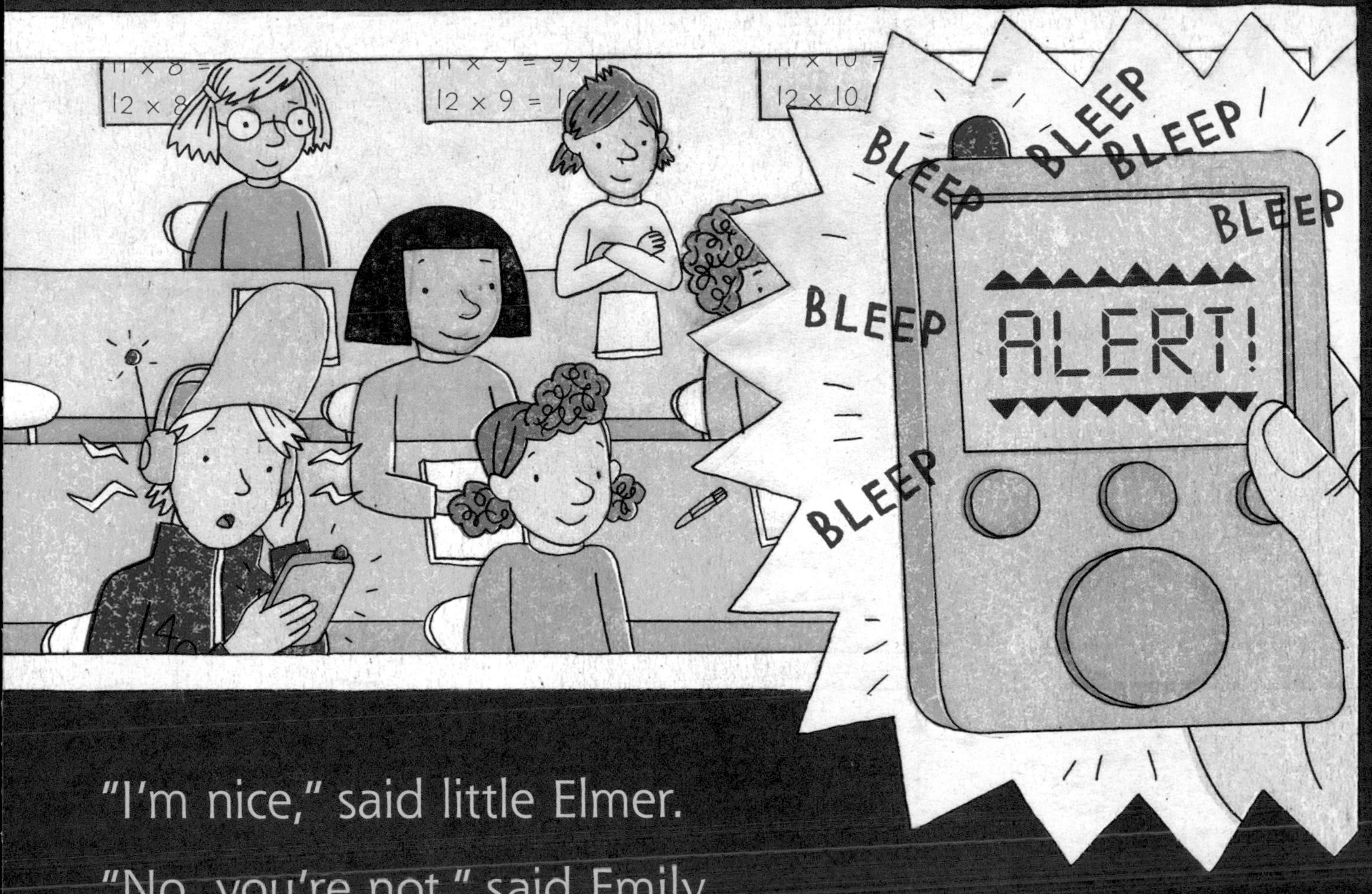

BLEEP
BLEEP
BLEEP
BLEEP
BLEEP
BLEEP
ALERT!

"I'm nice," said little Elmer.

"No, you're not," said Emily.

"I am, aren't I, Dad?"
said Elmer.

"You're both very
good," said Dad.

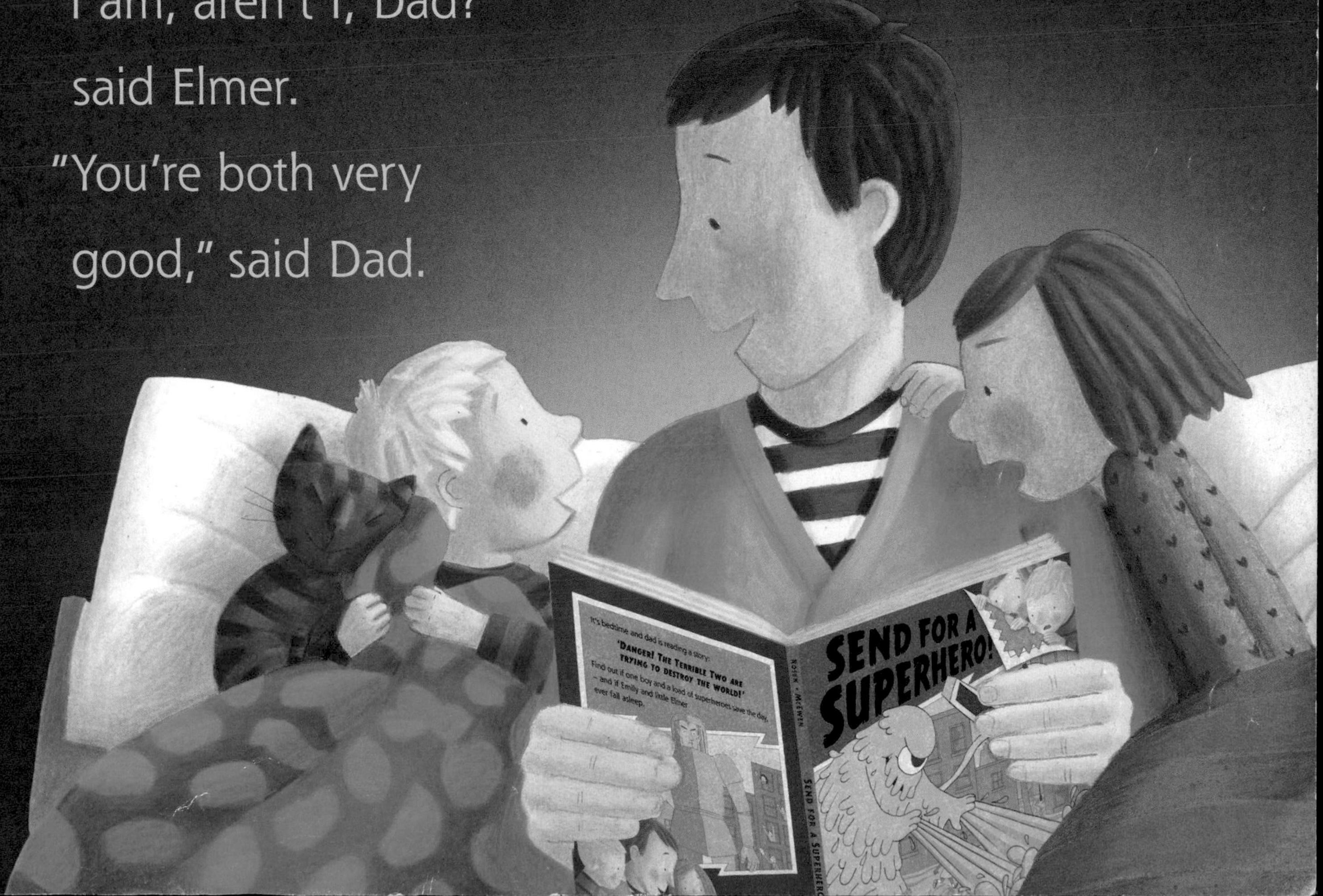

SEND FOR A SUPERHERO!

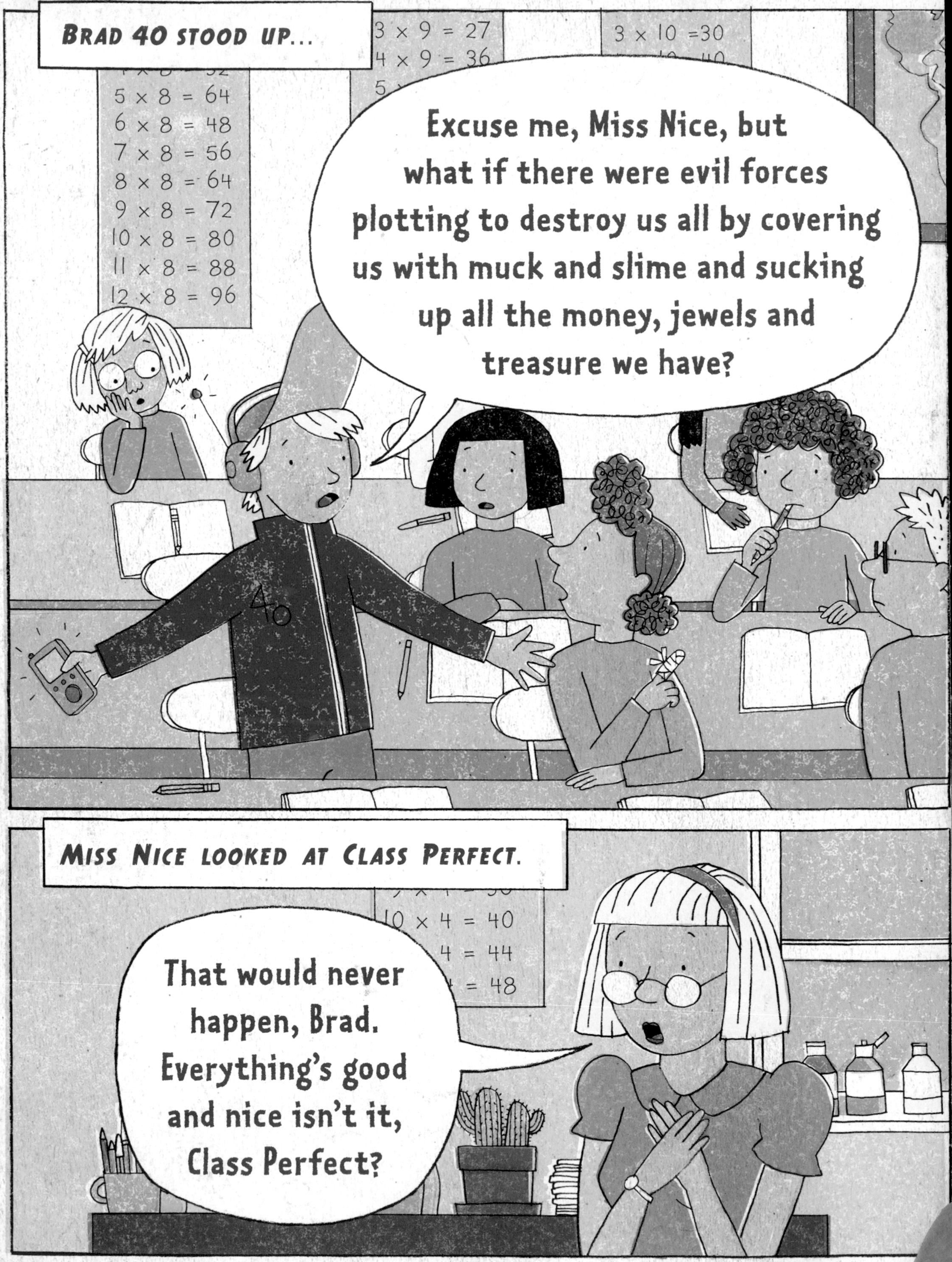
BRAD 40 STOOD UP...
3 × 9 = 27
4 × 9 = 36
3 × 10 = 30
5 × 8 = 64
6 × 8 = 48
7 × 8 = 56
8 × 8 = 64
9 × 8 = 72
10 × 8 = 80
11 × 8 = 88
12 × 8 = 96
Excuse me, Miss Nice, but what if there were evil forces plotting to destroy us all by covering us with muck and slime and sucking up all the money, jewels and treasure we have?
40
MISS NICE LOOKED AT CLASS PERFECT.
10 × 4 = 40
That would never happen, Brad. Everything's good and nice isn't it, Class Perfect?

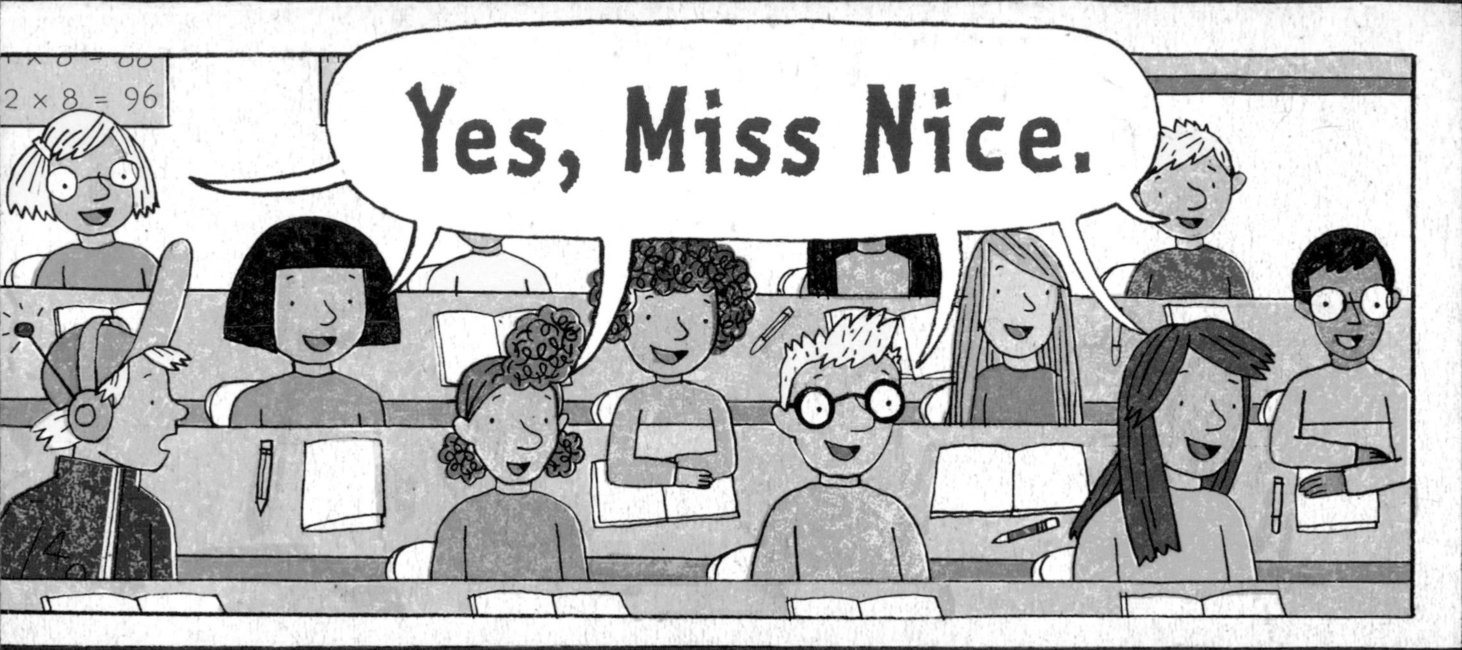
2 × 8 = 96
Yes, Miss Nice.

Emily said, "Brad 40 knows what's going on, doesn't he, Dad?"

Little Elmer jumped up.

"I'm Brad 40!"

"No, you're not," said Emily.

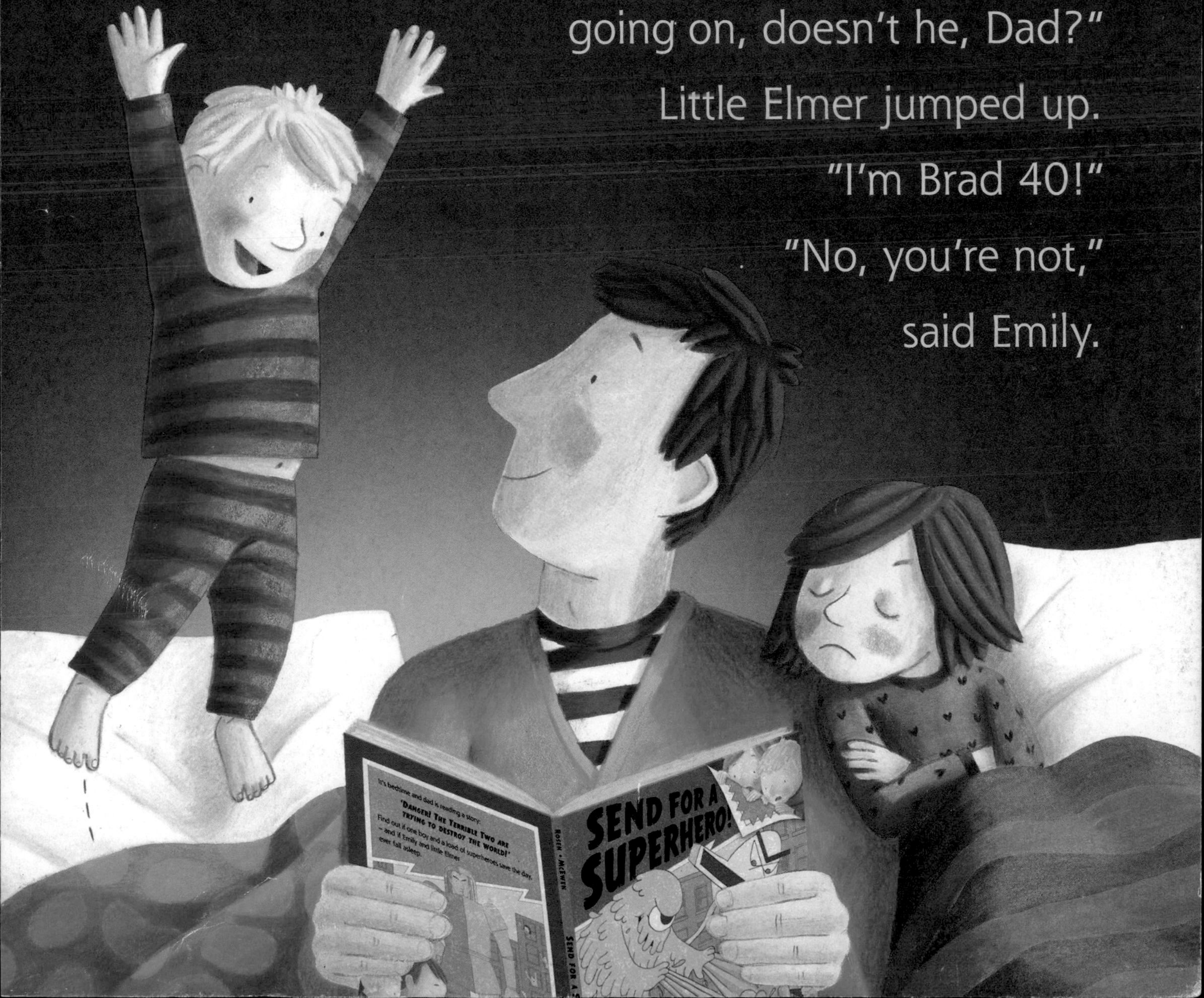
SEND FOR A SUPERHERO!

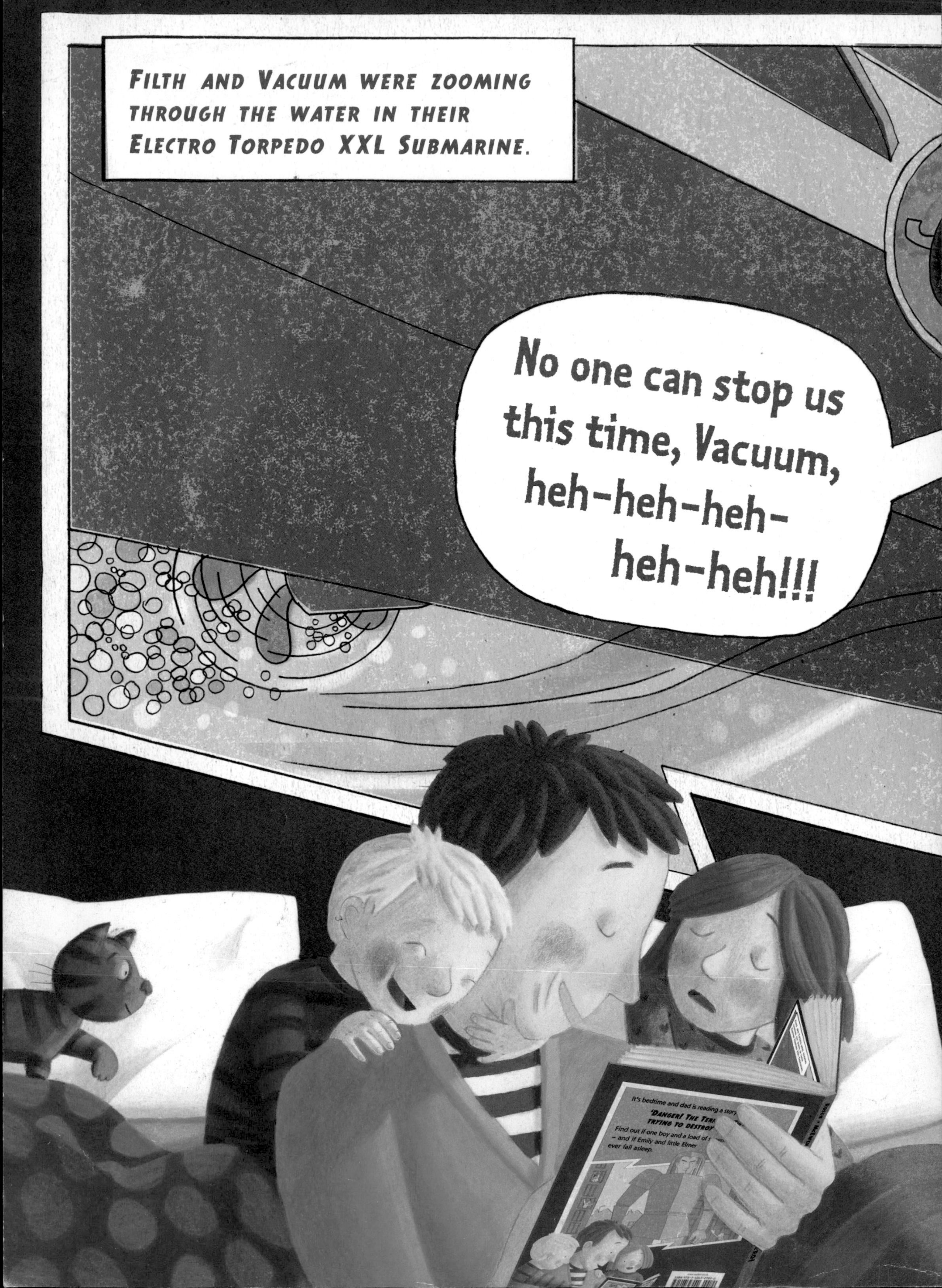
FILTH AND VACUUM WERE ZOOMING THROUGH THE WATER IN THEIR ELECTRO TORPEDO XXL SUBMARINE.
No one can stop us this time, Vacuum, heh-heh-heh-heh-heh!!!

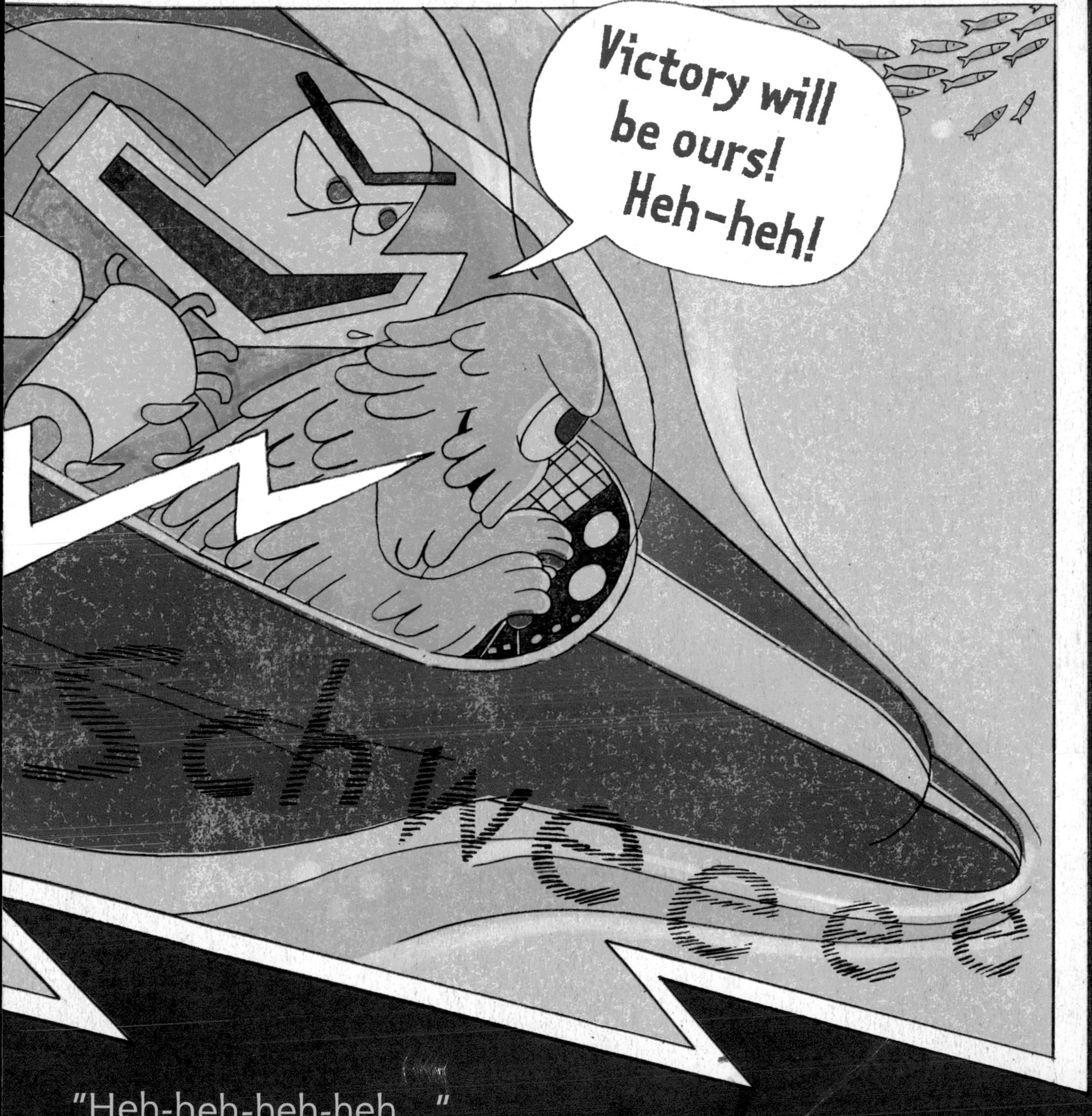
Victory will be ours! Heh-heh!
Schweeeee

"Heh-heh-heh-heh..."

"Enough cackling, thanks Dad," said Emily.

"Heh-heh-heh-heh-heh!" said little Elmer.

"No more cackling now, thanks Elmer," said Emily.

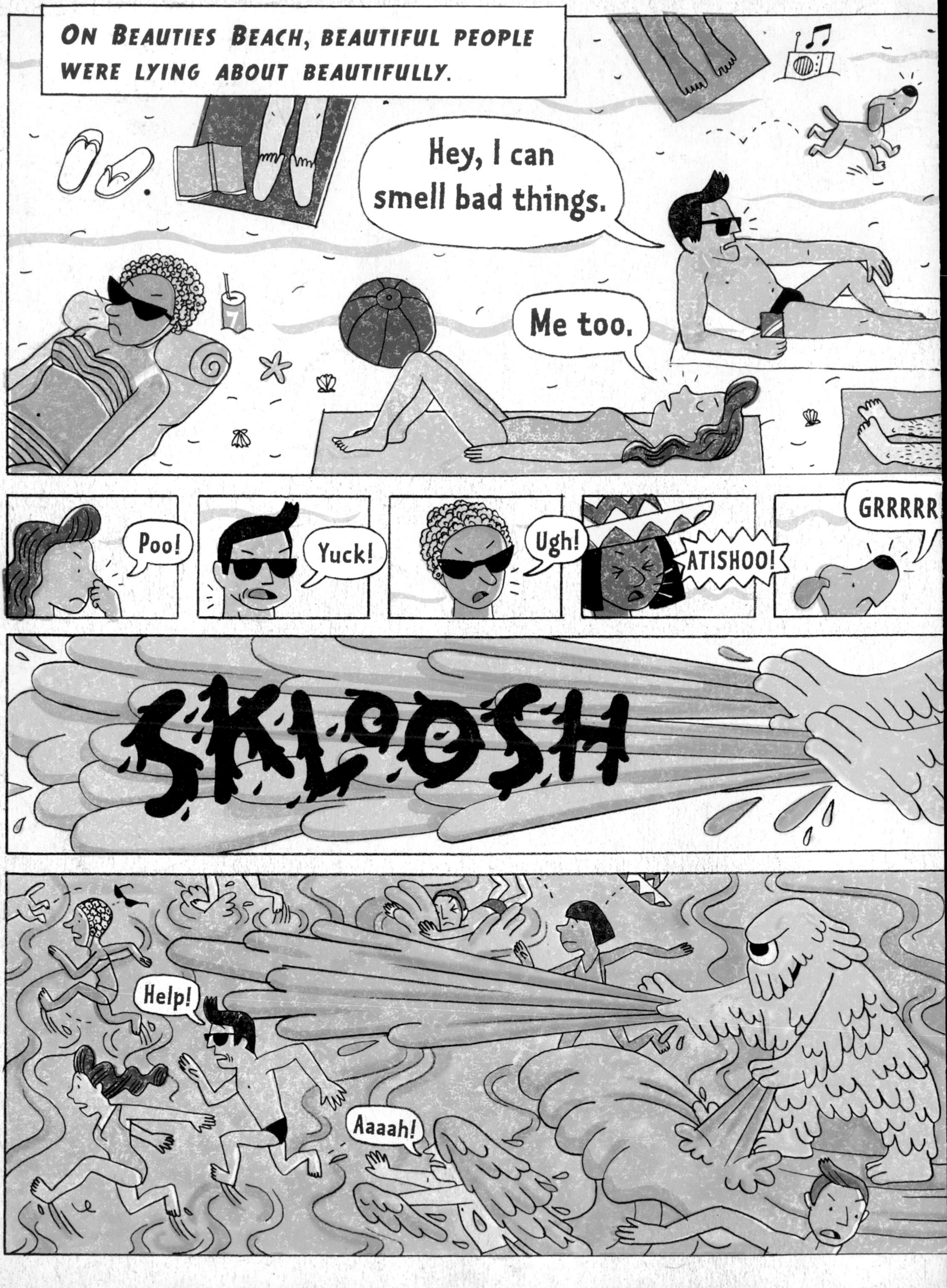
ON BEAUTIES BEACH, BEAUTIFUL PEOPLE WERE LYING ABOUT BEAUTIFULLY.
Hey, I can smell bad things.
Me too.
Poo!
Yuck!
Ugh!
ATISHOO!
GRRRRR
SKLOOSH
Help!
Aaaah!

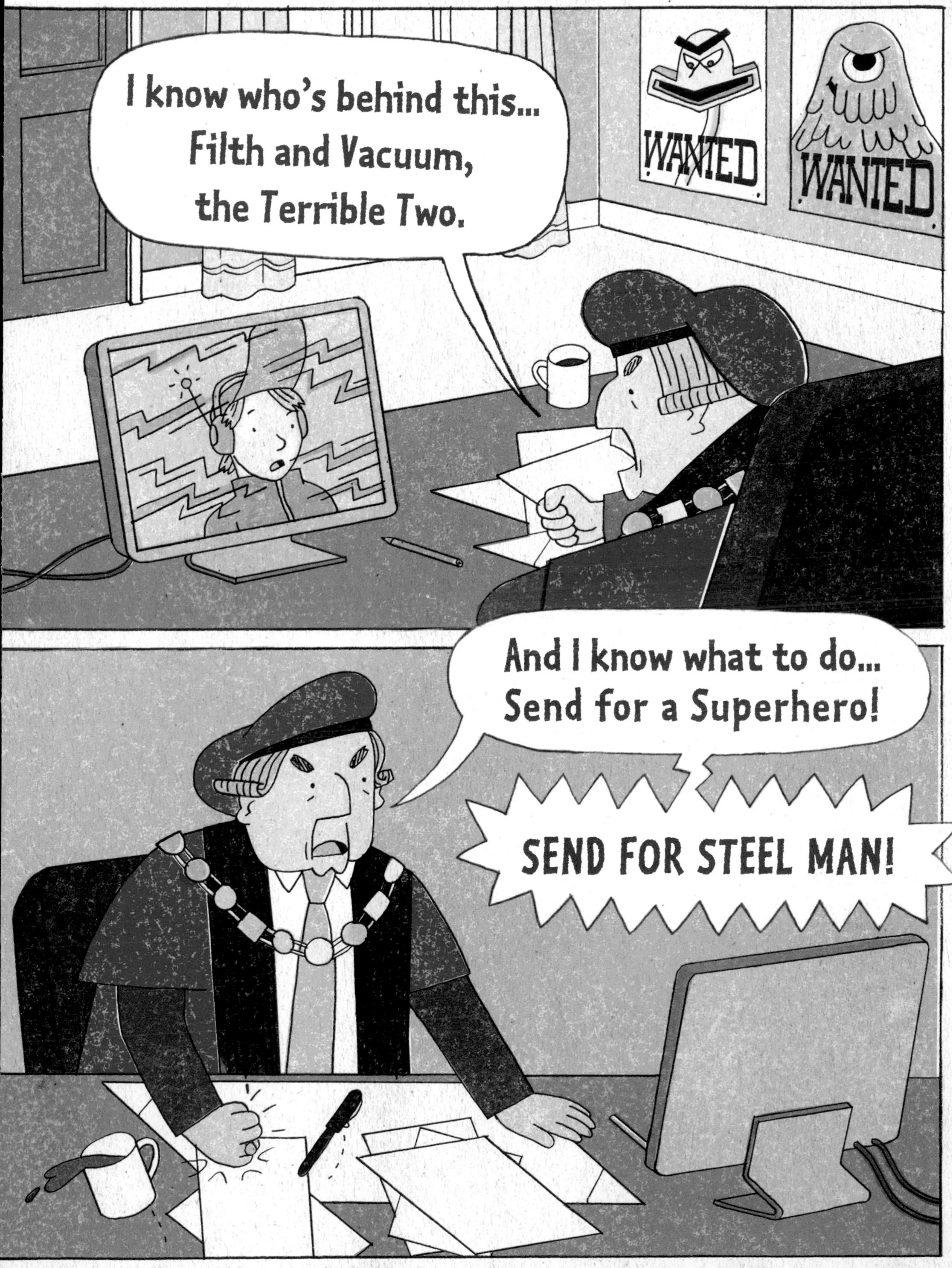

I know who's behind this... Filth and Vacuum, the Terrible Two.
WANTED
WANTED
And I know what to do... Send for a Superhero!
SEND FOR STEEL MAN!

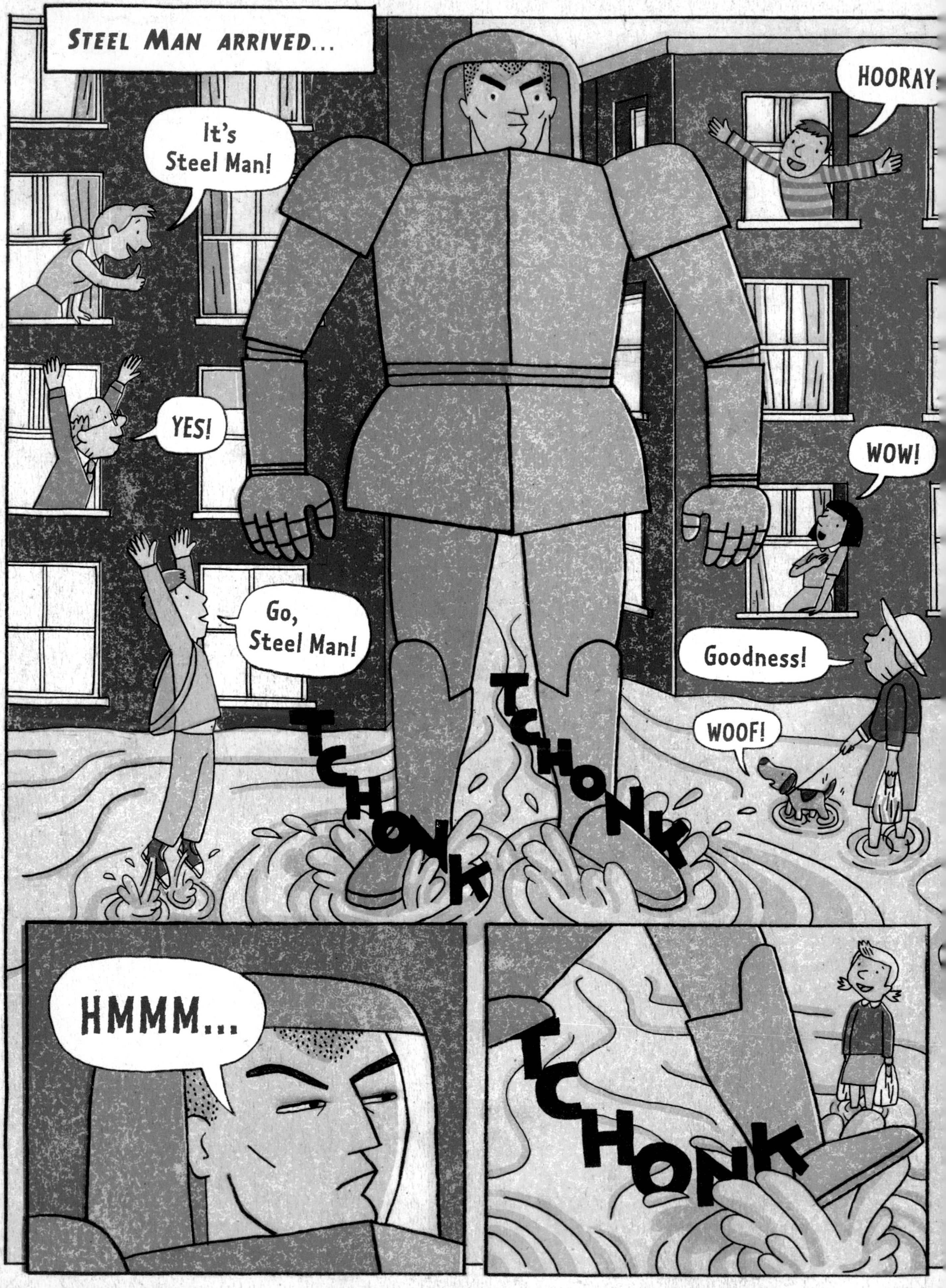
STEEL MAN ARRIVED...
It's Steel Man!
HOORAY!
YES!
WOW!
Go, Steel Man!
Goodness!
WOOF!
TCHONK
TCHONK
HMMM...
TCHONK

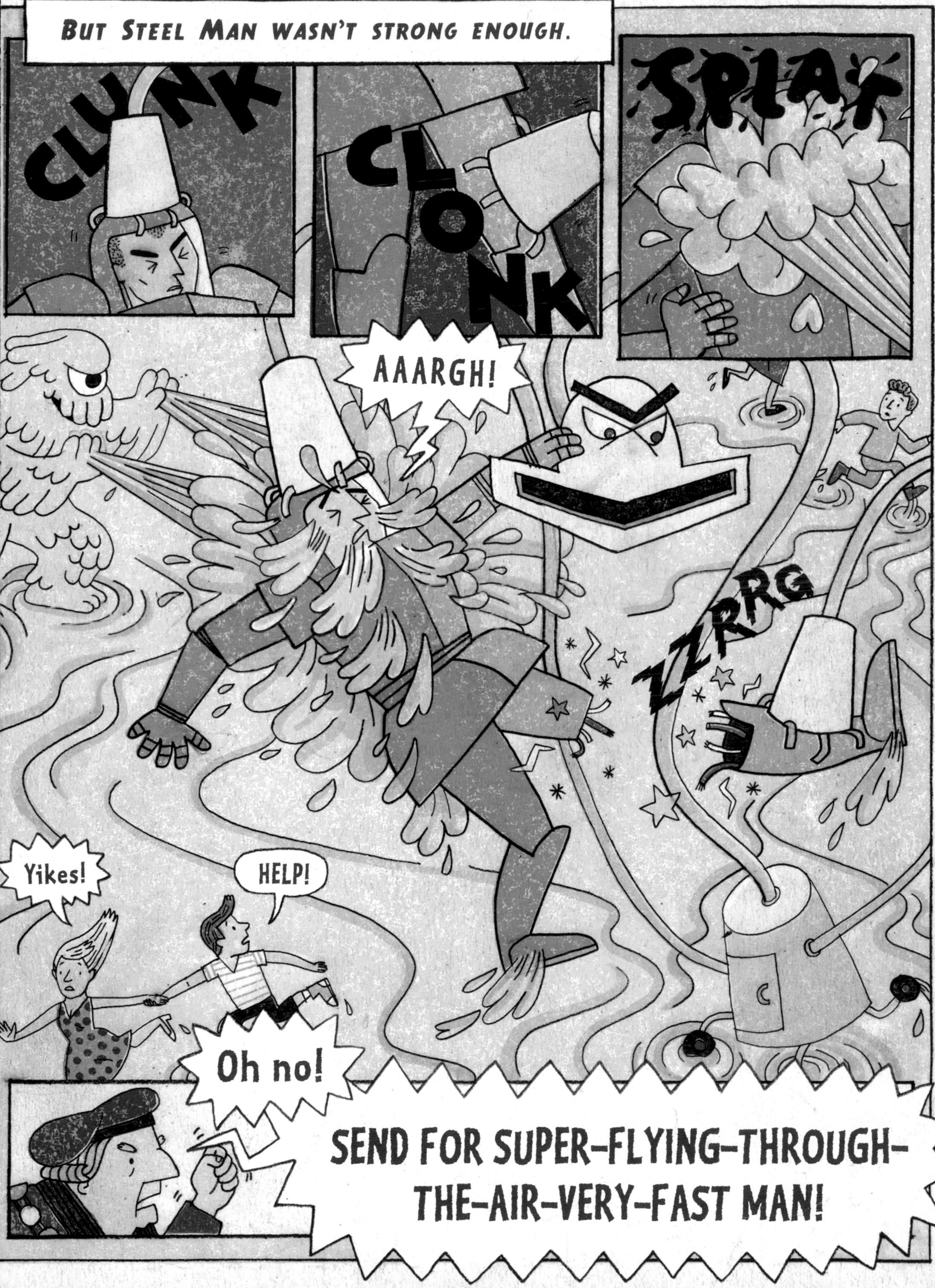

BUT STEEL MAN WASN'T STRONG ENOUGH.
CLUNK
CLONK
SPLAT
AAARGH!
ZZRRG
Yikes!
HELP!
Oh no!
SEND FOR SUPER-FLYING-THROUGH-THE-AIR-VERY-FAST MAN!

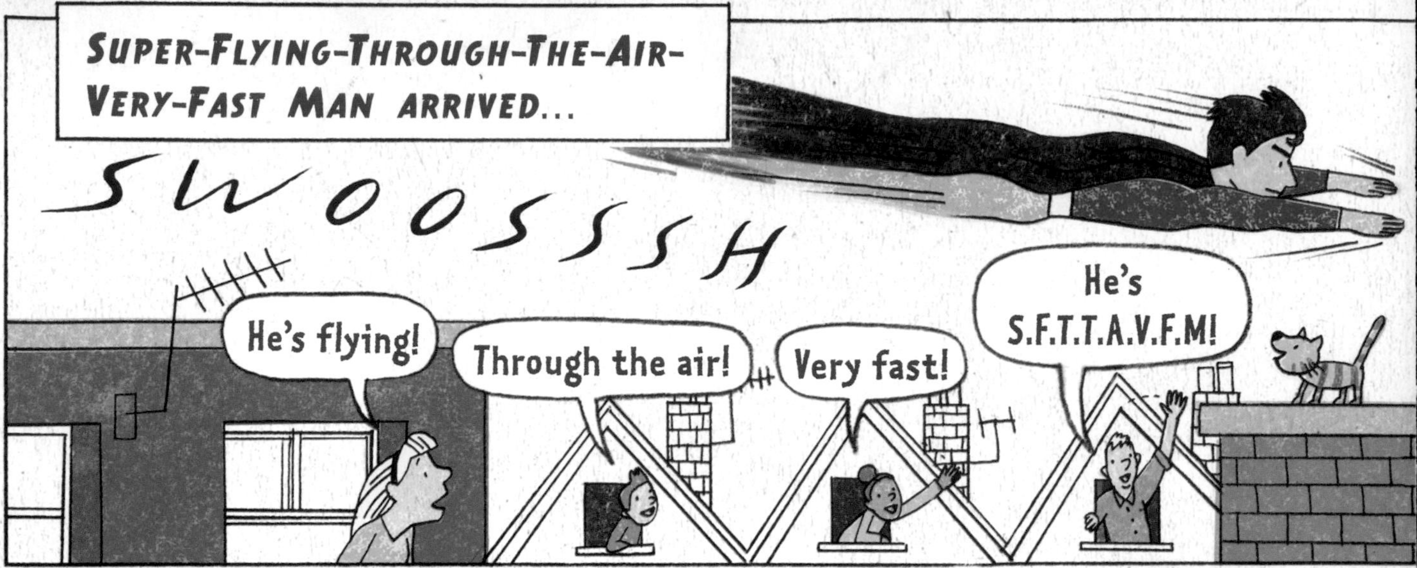
SUPER-FLYING-THROUGH-THE-AIR-VERY-FAST MAN ARRIVED...
SWOOSSSH
He's flying!
Through the air!
Very fast!
He's S.F.T.T.A.V.F.M!

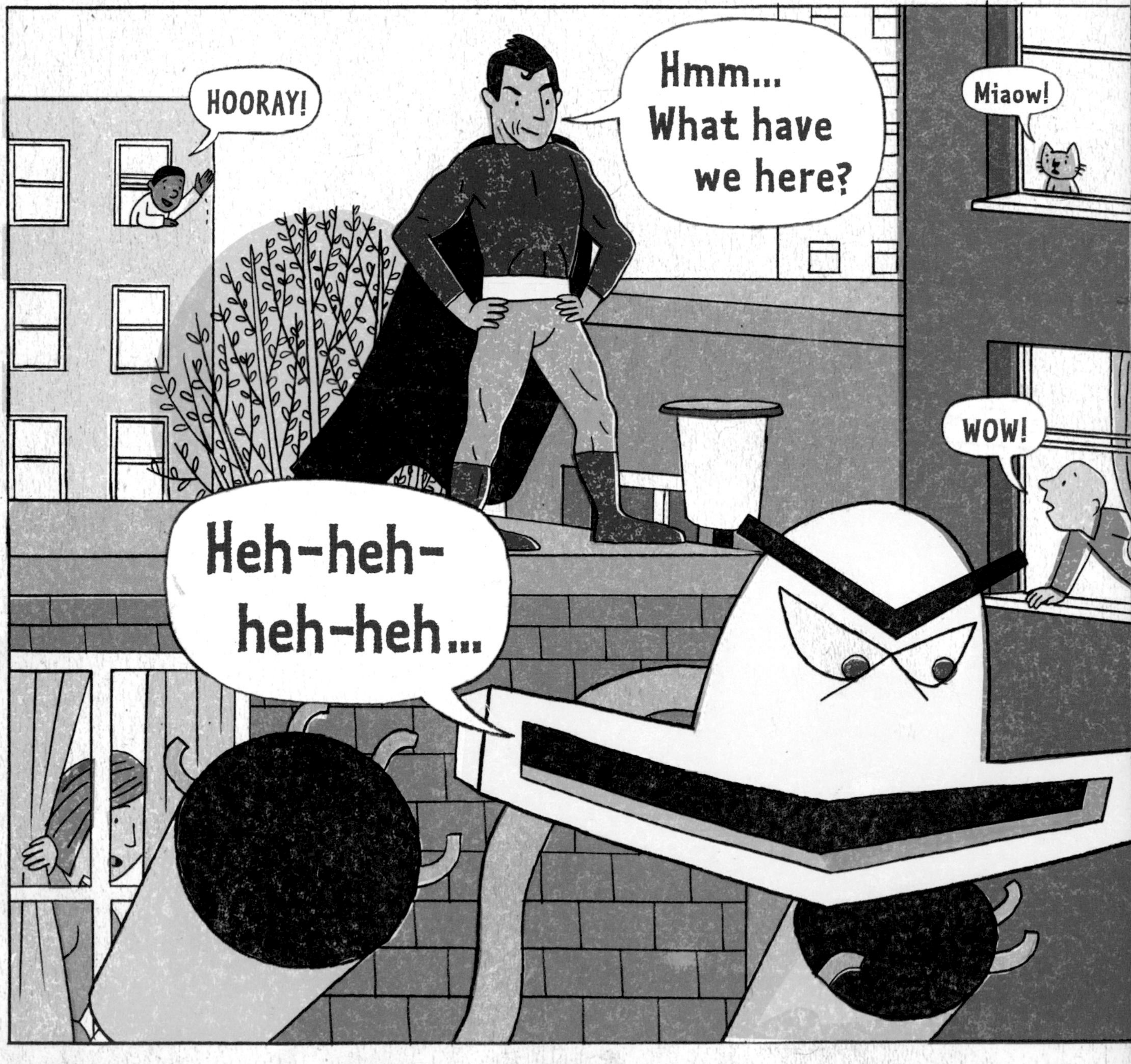
HOORAY!
Hmm... What have we here?
Miaow!
WOW!
Heh-heh-heh-heh...

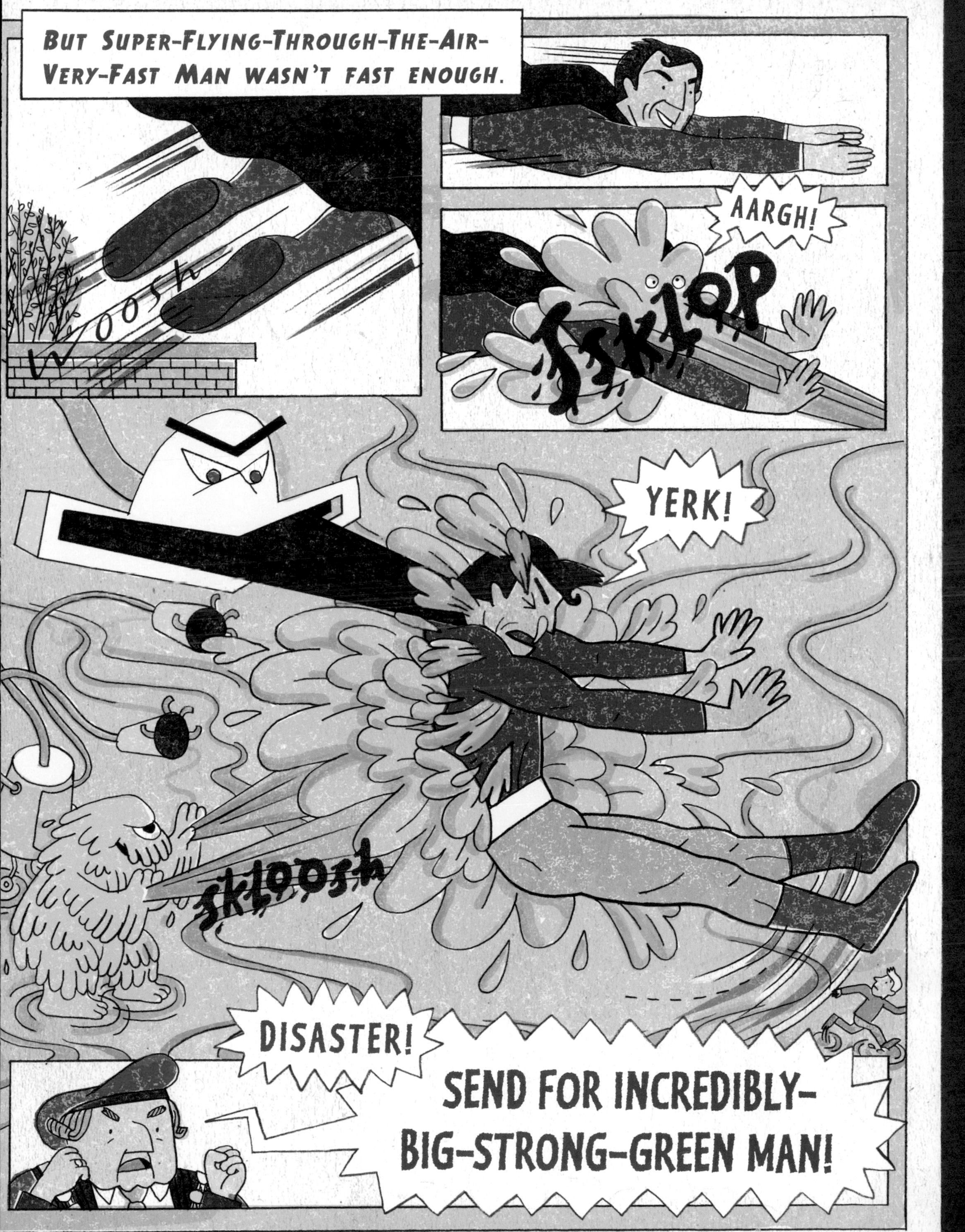
BUT SUPER-FLYING-THROUGH-THE-AIR-VERY-FAST MAN WASN'T FAST ENOUGH.
WOOSH
AARGH!
SKLOP
YERK!
SKLOOSH
DISASTER!
SEND FOR INCREDIBLY-BIG-STRONG-GREEN MAN!

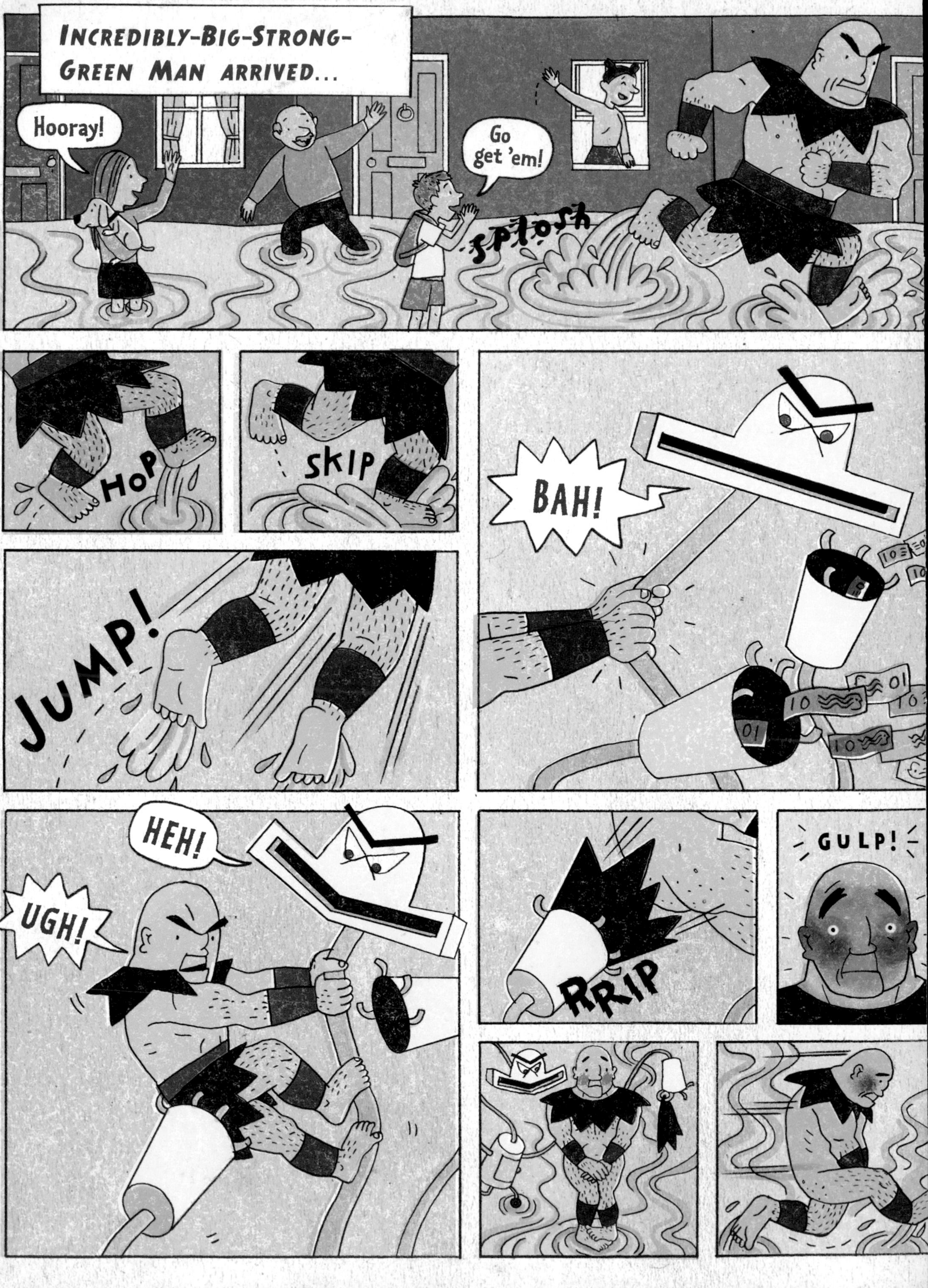

INCREDIBLY-BIG-STRONG-GREEN MAN ARRIVED...
Hooray!
Go get 'em!
SPLOSH
HOP
SKIP
BAH!
JUMP!
HEH!
UGH!
RRIP
GULP!

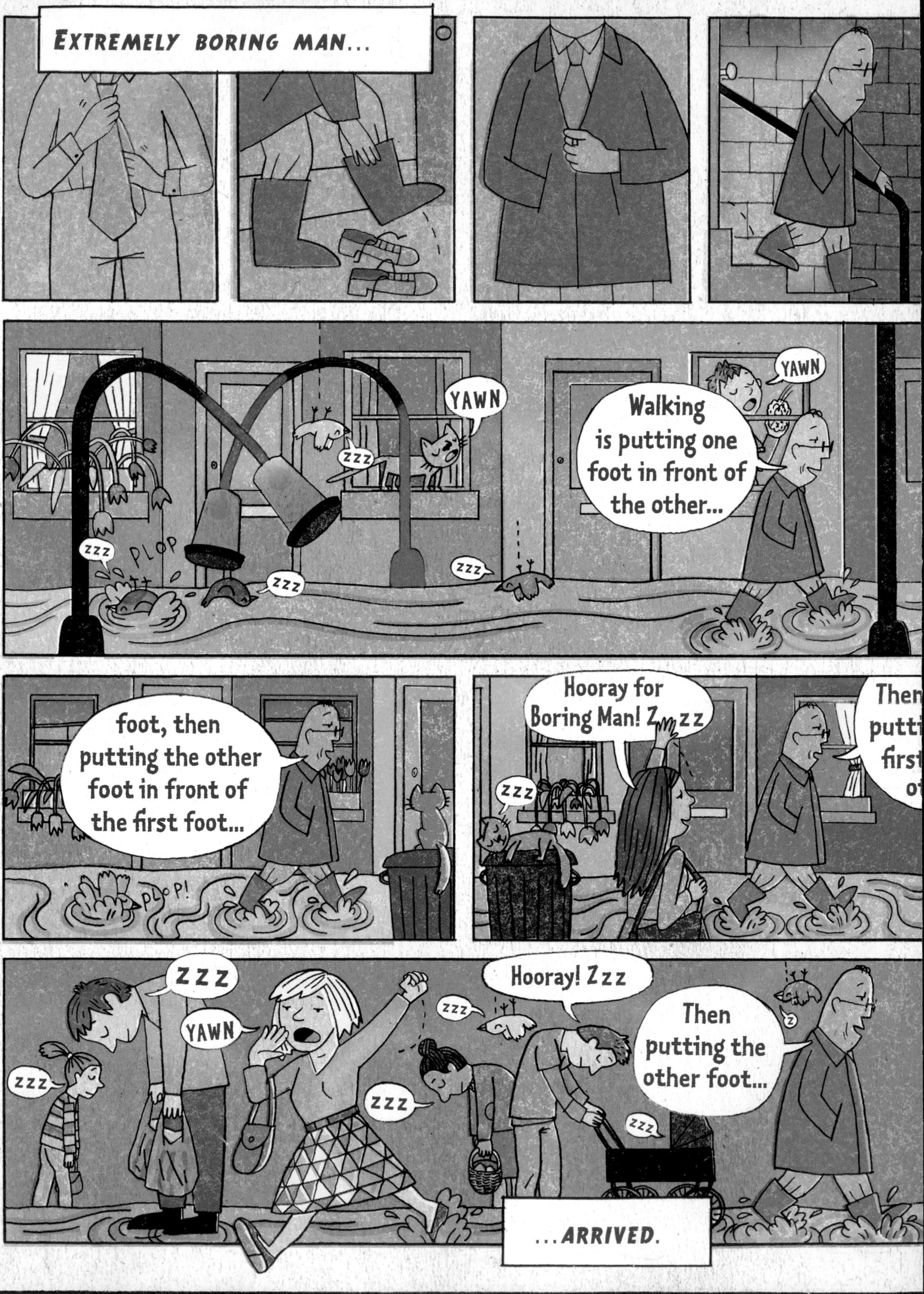
EXTREMELY BORING MAN...
YAWN
YAWN
Walking is putting one foot in front of the other...
ZZZ
ZZZ
PLOP
ZZZ
ZZZ
foot, then putting the other foot in front of the first foot...
PLOP!
Hooray for Boring Man! Z zz
ZZZ
Then
ZZZ
YAWN
ZZZ
ZZZ
Hooray! Zzz
ZZZ
Then putting the other foot...
ZZZ
...ARRIVED.

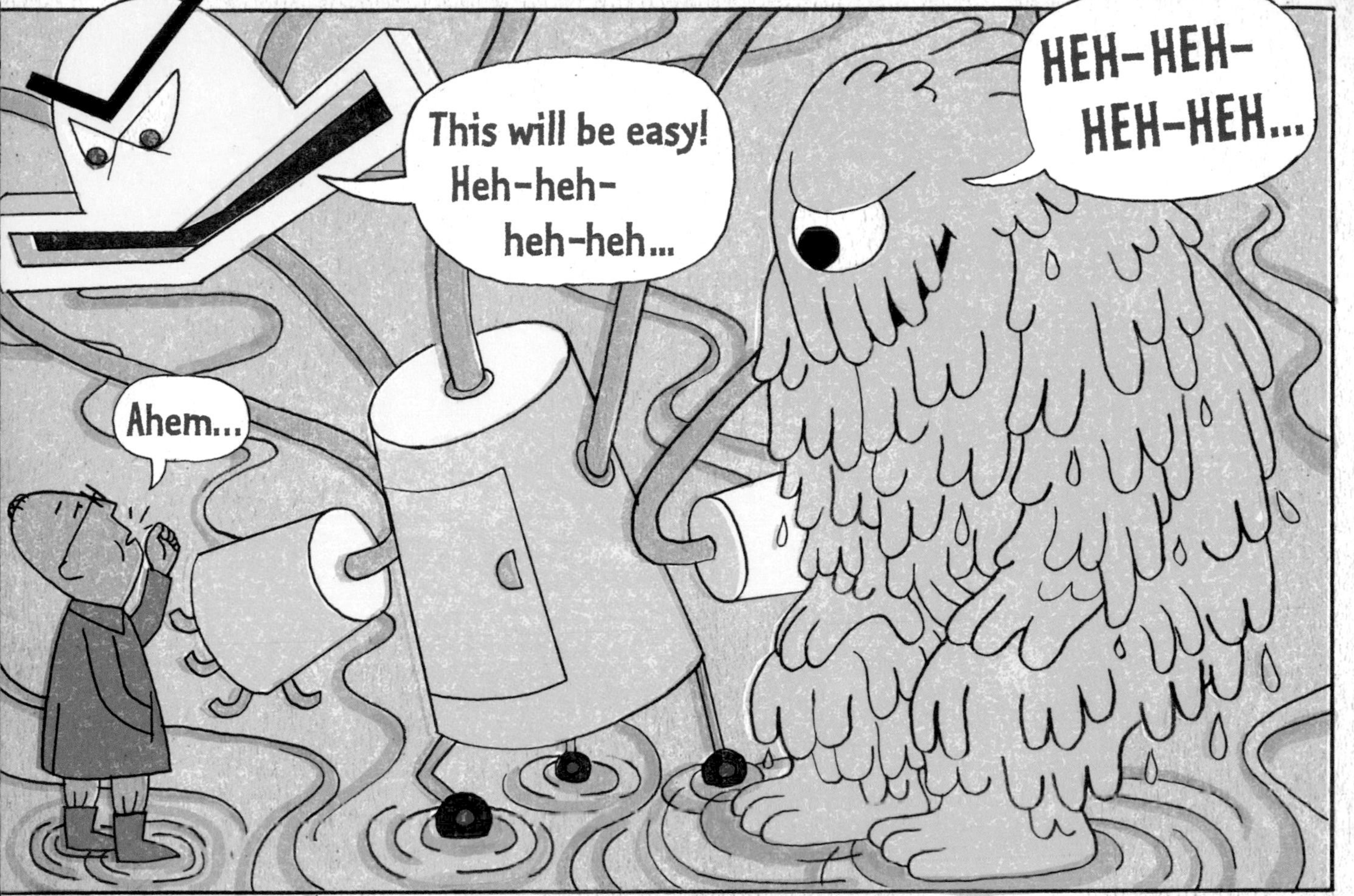
This will be easy! Heh-heh-heh-heh...
HEH-HEH-HEH-HEH...
Ahem...

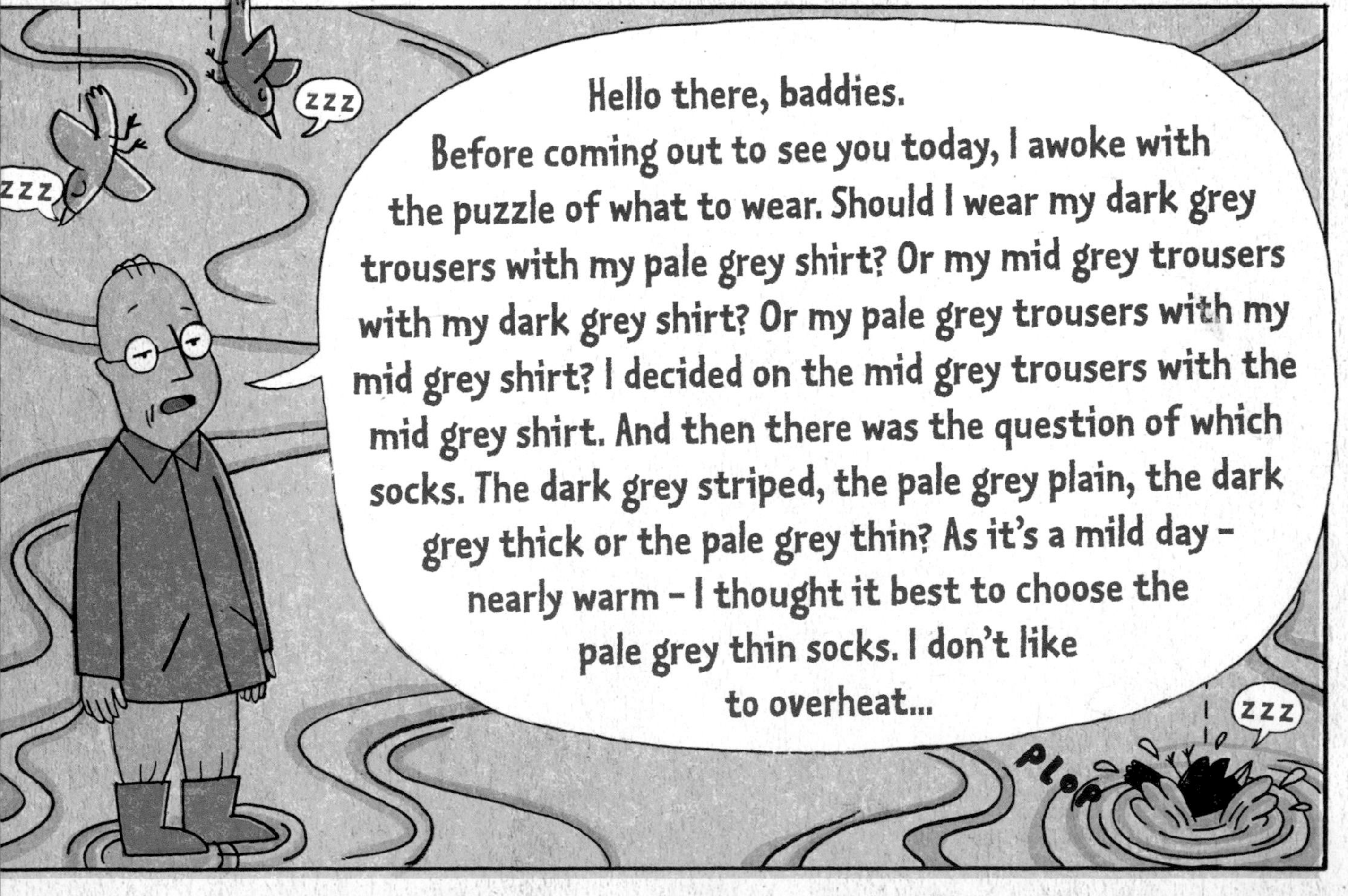
ZZZ
ZZZ
Hello there, baddies. Before coming out to see you today, I awoke with the puzzle of what to wear. Should I wear my dark grey trousers with my pale grey shirt? Or my mid grey trousers with my dark grey shirt? Or my pale grey trousers with my mid grey shirt? I decided on the mid grey trousers with the mid grey shirt. And then there was the question of which socks. The dark grey striped, the pale grey plain, the dark grey thick or the pale grey thin? As it's a mild day – nearly warm – I thought it best to choose the pale grey thin socks. I don't like to overheat...
ZZZ
PLOP

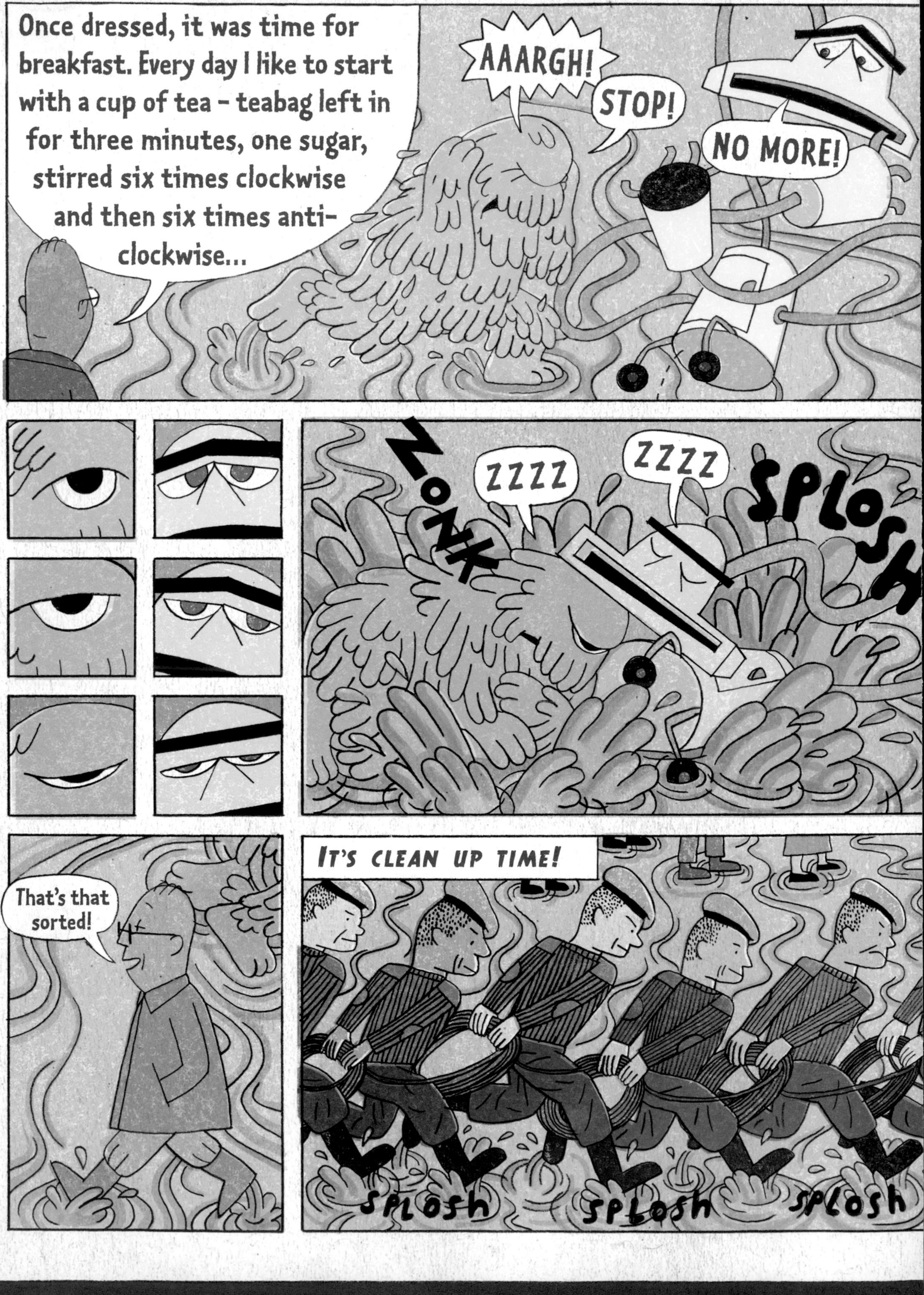
Once dressed, it was time for breakfast. Every day I like to start with a cup of tea – teabag left in for three minutes, one sugar, stirred six times clockwise and then six times anti-clockwise...
AAARGH!
STOP!
NO MORE!
ZONK
ZZZZ
ZZZZ
SPLOSH
That's that sorted!
IT'S CLEAN UP TIME!
SPLOSH
SPLOSH
SPLOSH

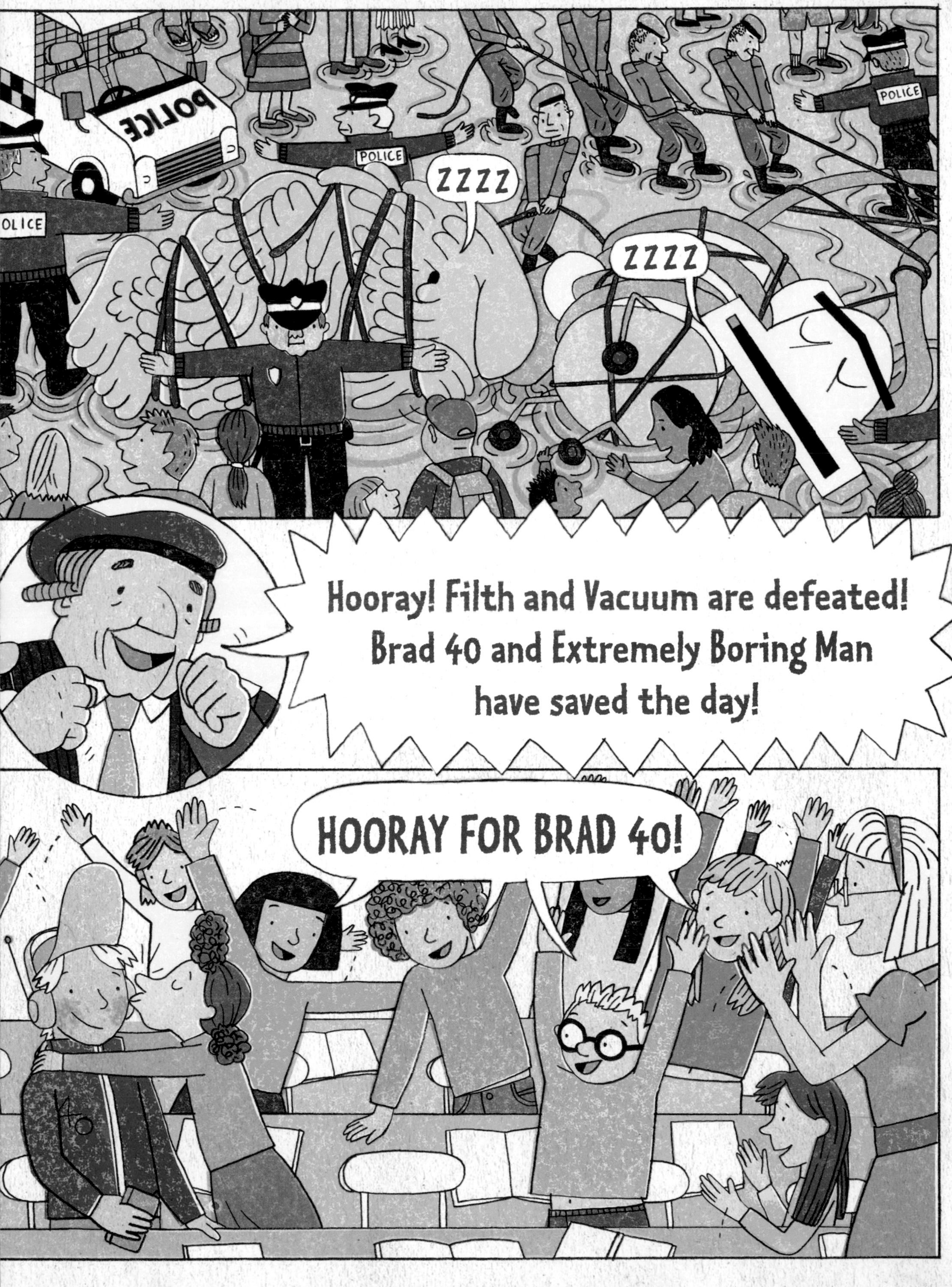
POLICE
POLICE
POLICE
OLICE
ZZZZ
ZZZZ
Hooray! Filth and Vacuum are defeated! Brad 40 and Extremely Boring Man have saved the day!
HOORAY FOR BRAD 40!

"And that," said Dad, "was how clever Brad 40 and Extremely Boring Man saved the world..."

Little Elmer and Emily lay in their beds sleeping soundly.

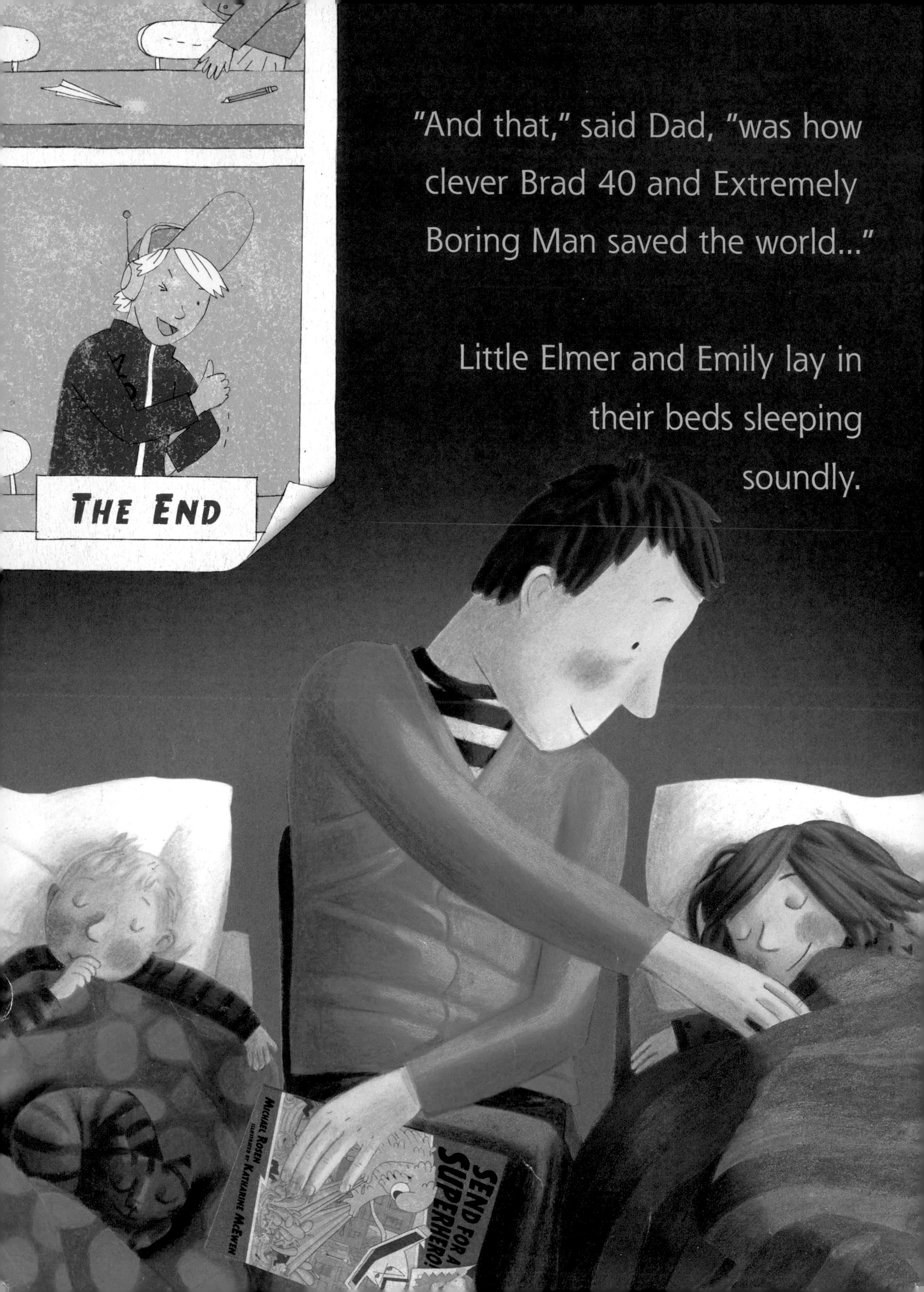
THE END
SEND FOR A SUPERHERO!
MICHAEL ROSEN
ILLUSTRATED BY KATHARINE McEWEN

Dad crept out of the room.
Mum had been listening
at the door.
"Are they asleep?"
"Oh, yes,"
said Dad proudly.

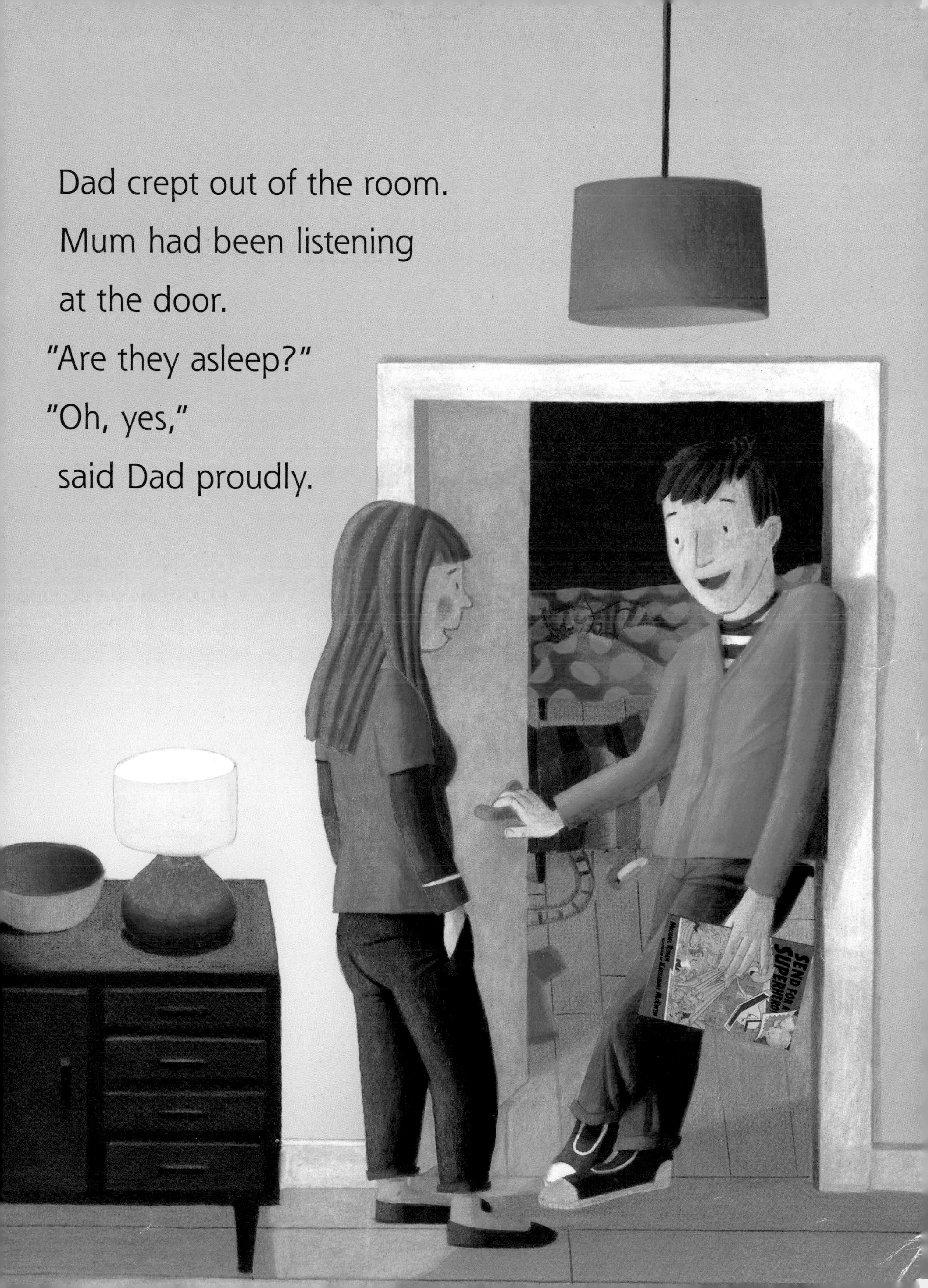
SEND FOR A SUPERHERO

"OH NO, WE'RE NOT!" shouted Emily and little Elmer from the bedroom.

"WE TRICKED YOU!"

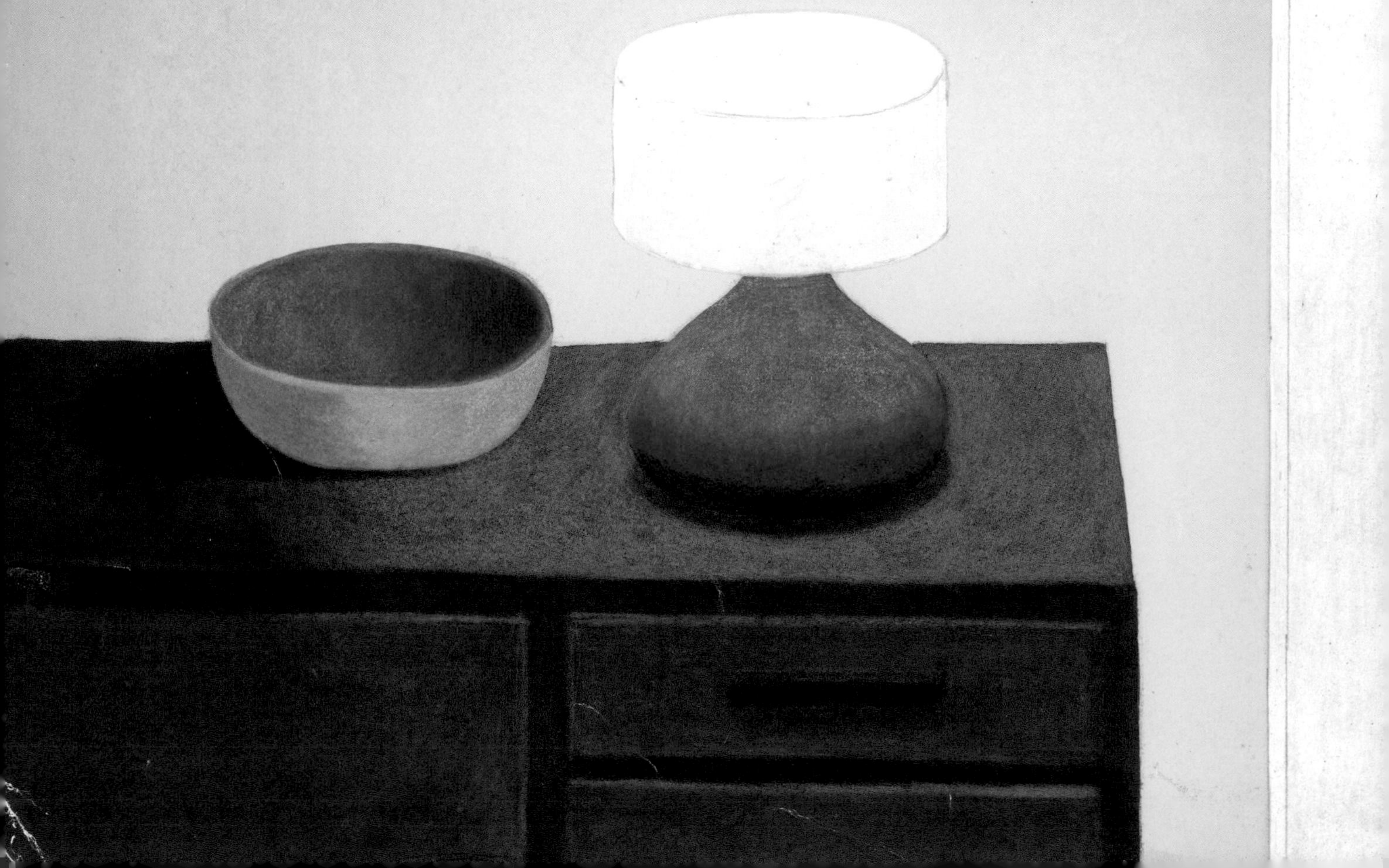

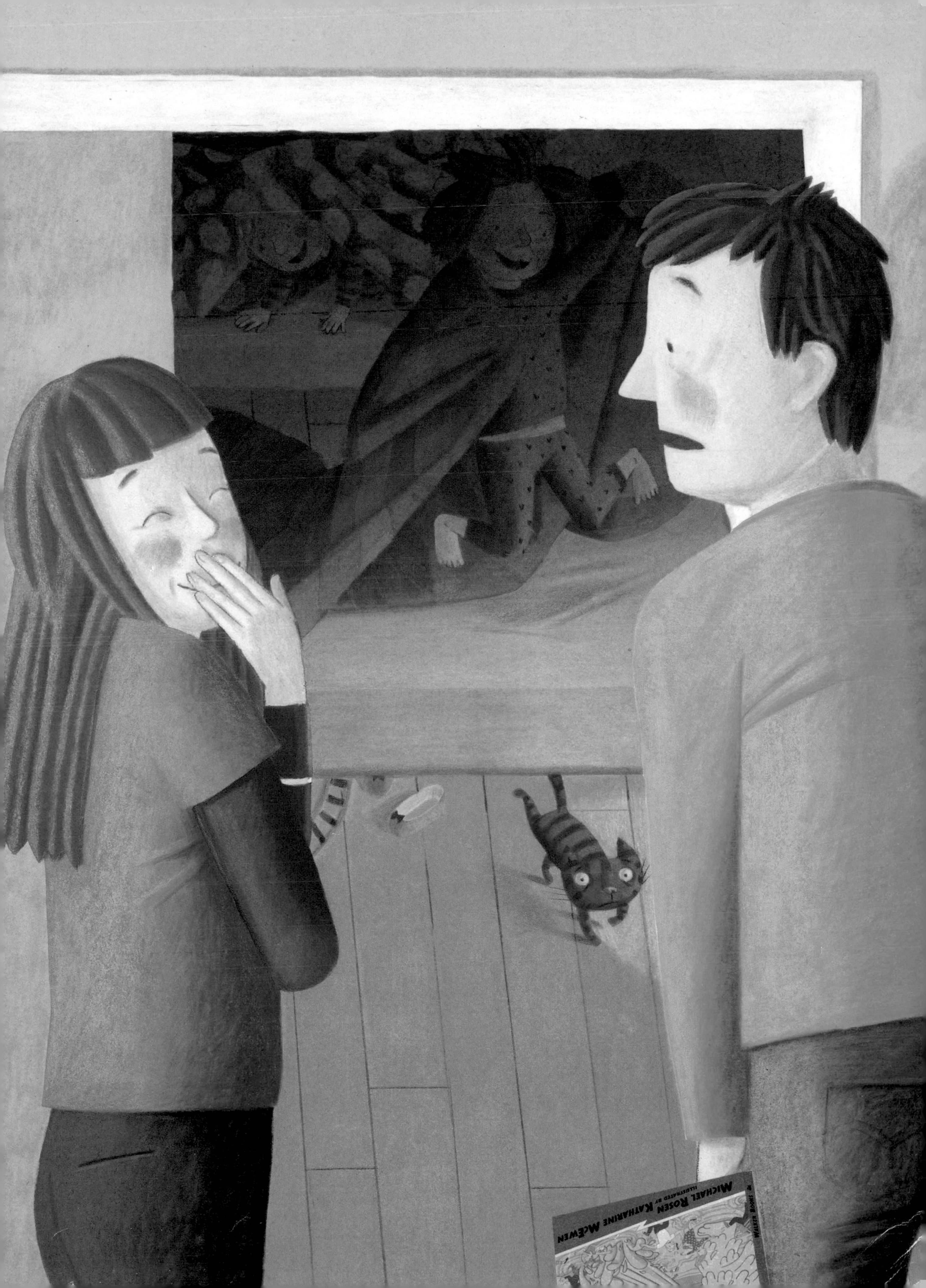
MICHAEL ROSEN
ILLUSTRATED BY
KATHARINE McEWEN
WALKER BOOKS

And so Dad started on a new chapter
of how Brad 40 saved the world.
Again.

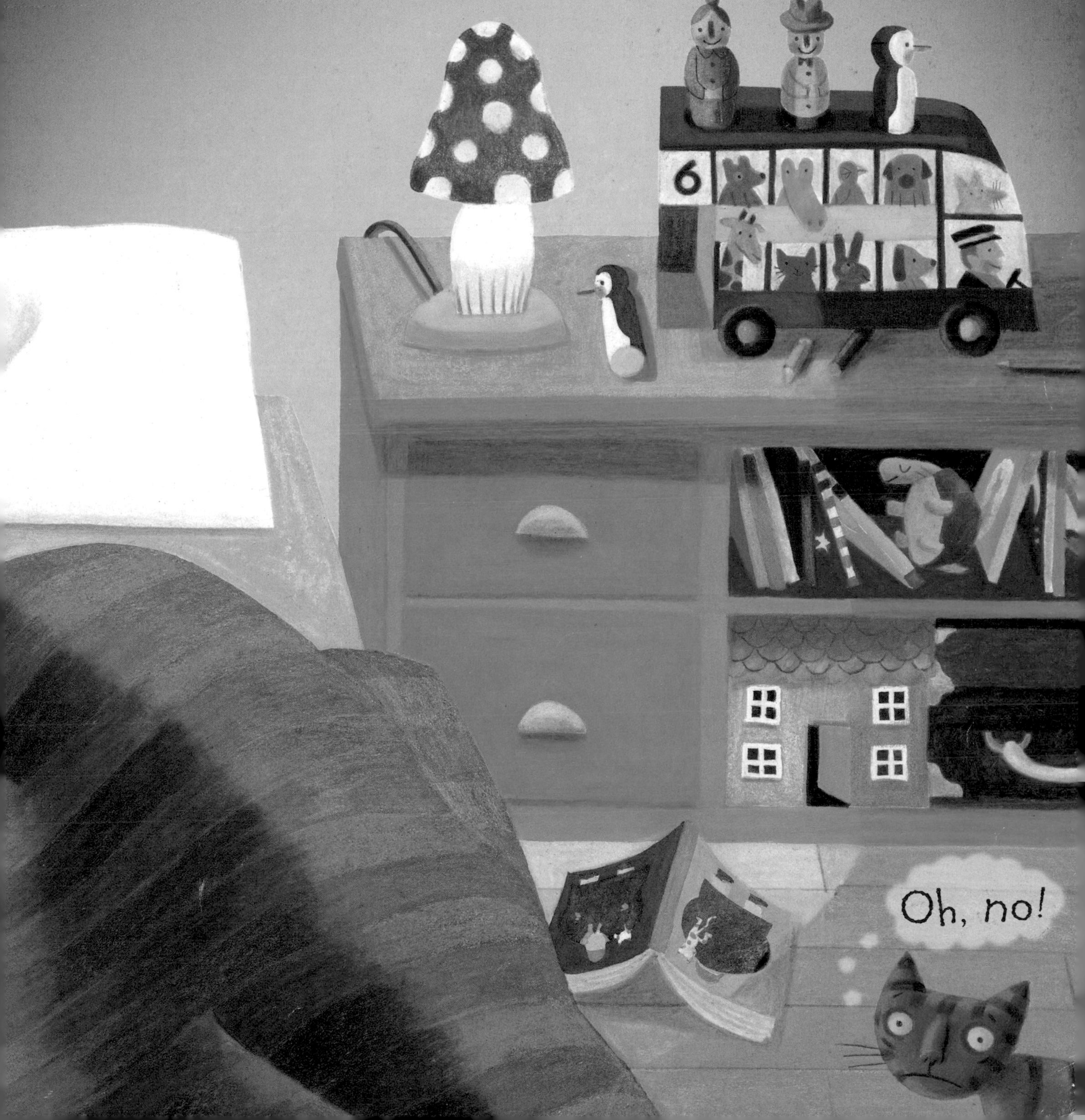
Oh, no!

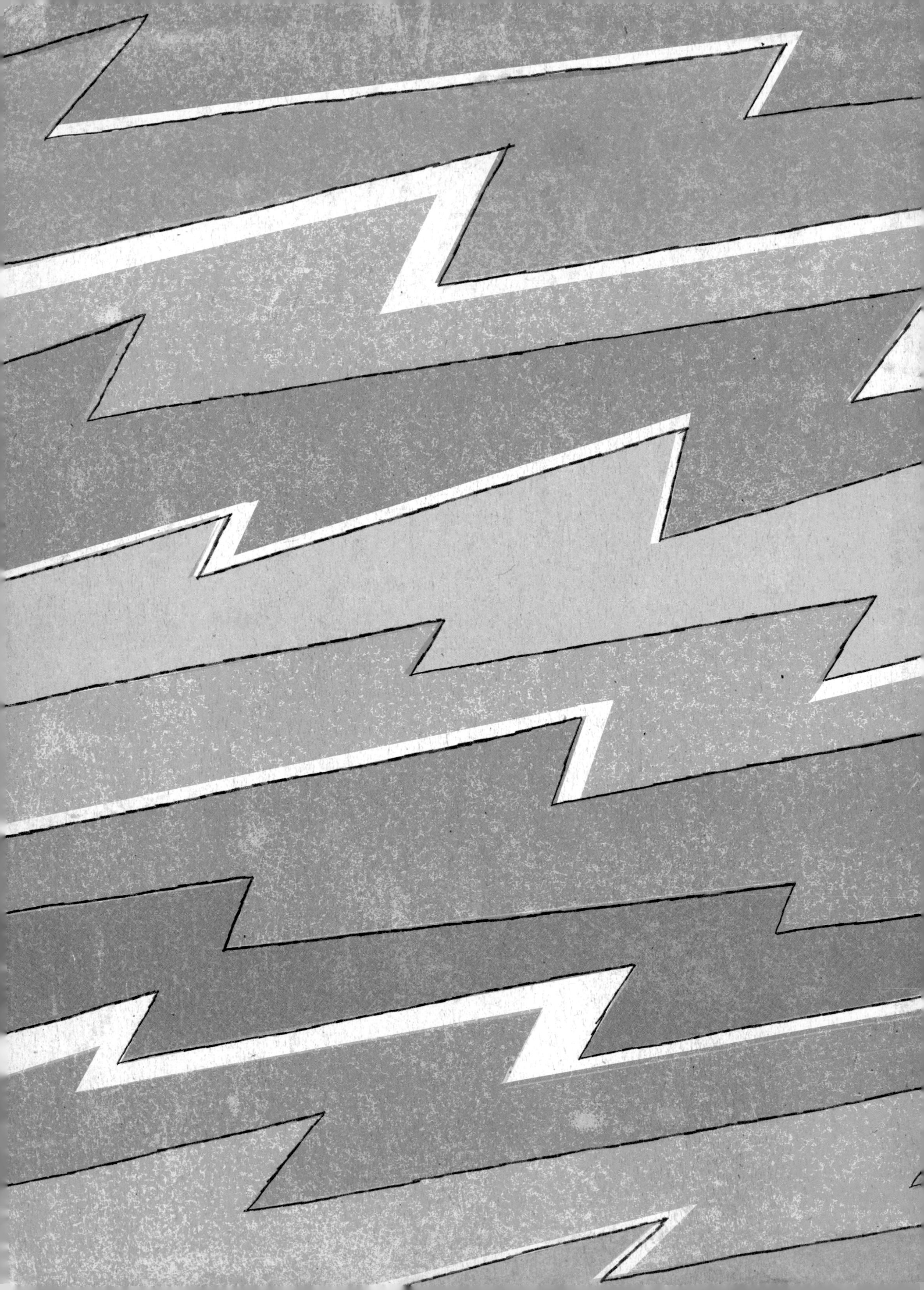